NOV   2013

The Mad Tibetan
stories from then and now

The Mad Tibetan

stories from then and now

AMARYLLIS

AMARYLLIS

AMARYLLIS

An imprint of Manjul Publishing House Pvt. Ltd.

Editorial Office:
J-39, Ground Floor, Jor Bagh Lane,
New Delhi 110 003, India
Tel: 011-24642447/24652447 Fax: 011-24622448
Email: amaryllis@amaryllis.co.in
Website: www.amaryllis.co.in

Registered Office:
10, Nishat Colony, Bhopal 462 003, M.P., India

ISBN: 978-93-81506-05-9

Printed and Bound in India by
Thomson Press (India) Limited

To,
My mother and father, for being who they are . . .

To Mama, for filling my childhood with stories from her life in
Burma; for introducing me to the art of story telling;
and to Piti, for instilling in me the discipline of keeping at it till
you get it *write* . . . .

To these two wonderful souls, I am forever indebted.

Contents

Acknowledgements

I'd like to thank my friend, Neeta Bakshi, for sharing with me a bitter-sweet memory from her childhood in Himachal;

Vas, a friend and filmmaker, for his candid recall of what he calls 'his first love', motivating me to write *Premonition*;

Jeffrey P. Pevelka of Mexico City, for his heartening reactions to my interpretation of the life of our dear friend, Ruth Mayberry;

I'd like to thank Phonsok Ladakhi, a friend and colleague from Leh, for his hospitality, and for making possible my encounter with the 'Mad Tibetan'.

I'd like to thank my cousin Manisha Gangahar for her first look at my stories;

I'd like to thank Prakash Jha for his words....

And most of all, I'd like to thank my editor Sanjana for meticulously going through the manuscript over and over, over the phone — she sitting in her Jor Bagh office in Delhi and me in my Bombay home, both of us hustling at times, for *just that one word*....

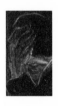

The Piano Tuner

His tall lanky figure stood stooped against the fading grey skyline of Bombay, a city that had woven itself around him like a cobweb. He shifted his gaze from the street below to the silhouette of the Taj hotel and beyond. The boats docked at the Gateway of India bobbed in the deluge. The rain had been incessant. Three days now he hadn't stepped out.

Feroze Batliboi turned his nodding head from the window to look at his inner world: a room — small, dark, un-candle-lit, redolent of un-played tunes. His piano, a deep rosewood, upright against the damp monsoon wall, glistened at the edges. He placed his finger on a G-major, tried to hold the key down; gentle, steady. The sound wobbled, tottered in the air.

Slivers of plaster bulged from the wall, their ends turned out like old wallpaper. On a small table — round and polished — sat conspicuously the black dial phone, holding a promise to ring. He looked at it awhile, and then looked away. From the shelf up on the wall he pulled out an old crimson diary, its leather frayed and discoloured. The old gnarled fingers uncurled the letter M, ran haphazardly down names in black and blue. One Mrs Mehta, a housewife from Santa Cruz had been learning to play the piano and had sent for him to come and tune the instrument regularly. There, right at the end of the page, after Max Mueller Bhavan and Manikchand, he saw the name, Mrs Mehta 'comma' Shyamalan. He will call her himself and remind her it was time she had her piano tuned. 6 — 4 — 8…1 — 7 — 1 — 4…the fingers moved jerkily; expectant.

'Hello,' answered a young ebullient voice.

'Is Mrs Mehta at home?'

'Oh, Mummy!…Please hold…Mummy is in the kitchen…Mummy! It's yawrr phooone…' And back into the receiver with animated breath, 'Who's calling?'

'I'm Feroze Batliboi…the piano tuner.'

'Whooo? What?' the thin voice trilled at the edge into a higher octave. Hmm…C-treble, Batliboi mused. Like mother, like daughter. Musical! She could perhaps grow up to be an opera singer if her mother encouraged her to pursue that direction.

'I'm Batliboi, the piano tuner.'

A metallic giggle at the other end….

'Mummy…it's the piano tuner…Mr Boy….' Another musical giggle and footsteps skidded off into the distance.

Feroze Batliboi held onto the receiver as one would hold an only source of light on a road map on a dark night. In the mirror that masked the left door of his cupboard he saw his reflection. A long, extremely prominent nose set itself apart on a gaunt geometric face; a nose that dived suddenly down at the tip without warning. His knees, like two fists, bulged from a pair of trousers. Sitting on the tiny stool next to the telephone, his figure seemed so…so doubled up. Double, he thought. Like double bass…or *double-step*.

His mom beckoning him from the window to pick up only the freshly baked loaf from Tushaar Manzil Bakery next to Colaba Post Office. And he'd run off across the street ducking and dodging trams and carriages of elegant phirang women riding Victorias. From all the way across the street at Piroja Court, he could hear his father playing the piano. Notes emanated from the fifth floor and wafted across to the fisherman's wharf. Melodies, old and precious, he'd play till late, when he'd have time for pure music; music for the sake of music, melody for the sake of melody; not for the sake of money. For money, he would go to people's homes and teach.

'Hello! Mr Batliboi! Mrs Mehta here. Well…err…I was going to call you myself, you see…I….'

Batliboi straightened up. 'I…called to ask if it would be alright with you that I came in tomorrow to tune the piano…has been months….'

'Oh, yes, but tomorrow…no, well, tomorrow is not such a good idea, you know tomorrow is my daughter's exam and she is so bad at math! Atrocious! I suppose if you came in tomorrow, then…you couldn't tune the piano without playing it. I mean you'd have to make all that noise, won't you? And the girl will get disturbed. It is her last paper…err…let me call you, Mr Batli, once I'm done with all this here.'

'Oh, not a problem at all…I can come…perhaps…the day after tomorrow,' Batliboi spoke anxiously, groping for words.

'No, no please! Not the day after! Day after tomorrow we are all leaving for Bangalore — Ooty, actually. Children's holidays begin, you see…not a day to waste here in Bombay!'

Feroze Batliboi shifted on his tiny stool.

'Mrs Mehta…you are keeping up your piano lessons, aren't you?'

'Of course! I love playing the piano! But you know what? Every time I sit down to play it, my little one, na? He will come…and go bang-bang-bang on it! He awl-ways wants to play it himself.'

She chuckled proudly. 'And my husband, na! Oh god! He tells me I look best in the kitchen. And he will butt in and start playing all those Hindi filmy songs! Like a harmonium, you know? With one hand only! My god! I never get any time to myself. Something or the other always going on here! But I'll call you, *haan*? After the vacation is over…and then get serious about my piano playing. Let me get a little free! Thank you for calling, Mr Batli…so sweet you remembered…thank you, Byii!'

Feroze Batliboi sagged on his stool. Mrs Mehta's words ran into each other like an eggbeater pressed down so there were no spaces left for doubt. It was clear. She was *not* interested in continuing with her piano lessons so she didn't need a piano tuned. Five hundred rupees gone, right there. Just like that. It could have taken care of the BSES bill at least. He placed the receiver down like someone closing a road map after realising his destination was not shown on it.

He'd have to think. Who else? Who else needed a piano tuned? He was peering at his own image in the mirror. Batliboi shook his head, the long white hair tousled, hanging wet against his sunken face. He slow-turned-around on the stool and stood up on his feet. The kids next-door shrieked in front of video games. He walked across to the old chaise lounge next to the almirah, and sank into it. Overcome with torpor, Batliboi closed his eyes, breathing heavily. His hands lay on his bony thighs in a perpetual state of tremor. The room, he noticed, had started to reek of *has beens*. The clock on the wall, the shoe rack with his old worn out Hush Puppies jutting out, his black umbrella, the beret his father left him, which whenever he wore, made people smile unintentionally at him.

He shuffled slowly towards the piano, placed his right hand on the lid and lifted it. *T o n g g g*…! One finger on the upper octave reverberated in the small, well-kept room. *B h o o m*! A lower-than-low note challenged the gaiety of the first one. Then looking at the boats beyond the Gateway, his palm flat on the keyboard, he held down the sound of his pounding heart. Sometimes the palpitations became wild. He needed to sit, calm himself down, and think straight. Who, who in this rainy season, when everything around was rusting and rotting, would need to have a piano fine-tuned?

Ah…to fine-tune a piano…to drift slowly and melodiously from one key to another…to place those long veined fingers, sure and gentle on the glazed whites and lift them off at once — staccato!...holding them in the air, the notes resonating. Press them down hard again, as lightly, then let go. His fingers would move like water, creating ripples in the air...a brilliance, attributed only to him.

Eyes closed, he would play with gusto and then swirl around to look at her. Those eyes across the room, watching him, mesmerised by him, wanting, only him.

The lady would come to the bar with her Merchant Navy husband and sit sad-eyed, waiting for him to play. And once he swirled around on that stool, his wild locks falling over his moist brow, those eyes would begin to change. It was wartime. The Japanese invasion of Burma had sent many young girls into bars looking to feed their families. And she'd be there every evening. He could never forget those eyes, liquid eyes, forever changing...changing colour with each note that he played.

And then she was gone...gone....

He was not going to drift into spaces that were dark; crevices of his life, plastered and camouflaged. It is now, the now. He is living in the year two thousand nine. An old man, a *has been* pianist afflicted with Parkinsons...getting worse by the day. He can no longer play or teach. Thirteen years now he's only been tuning pianos. And now, even that seems remote.

He remembered the first time the keys had started to tremble beneath his fingers, he'd been startled. Politely they had told him:

'It's okay, Mr Batliboi, we'll find someone else.'

He'd come back home that evening, placed his right hand on the score and watched the pages underneath his touch, begin to rustle. He couldn't believe it. He must be nervous, stressed out obviously. He could do with a cup of tea, learn to relax. After all, he *was*

getting old now, his body needed the rest. He'd gone into the kitchen and put the kettle to boil. A fine brew from England that one of his students insisted on sending to him every year. He sat down on the chaise lounge and looked out at the boats plying between the Gateway and Alibagh. These last few days had been hectic. He needed to unwind. Eyes closed, he breathed deep, taking in the air from the sea....That's when he heard it...sure and steady...the sweet, faint clatter of china constant between his fingers, almost like a chime. He had looked down at his hands in horror. The pulsating was steady, rhythmic, a deafening sound! He had never noticed it. How long had it been there? Did everyone around him know? Is that why all his tuitions had fizzled out one after the other? His world shook. A pianist, with hands that...*moved*!

If only his fingers could be steady. Could hold a key down to its infinity, till the end of its echo...steady...till...! He had learnt to feign concentration. Pretend the trembling was part of *fine tuning*. They'd even nod at his virtuosity, with expressions of 'yes...it's getting there...yes...almost perfect....' But only he knew and only he suffered the agony of a note. Only he could feel the pain of sound. He struggled for stillness, yearned for that *one* silence that lay beyond the echo of each melodious note. He had to do it, had to get it right, and all he had, was his hands.

The pulsating had come to stay. He could no longer hold down the notes at his beck and call. He thought of the two boys from the famous business family — the Mirchandanis on Walkeshwar Road. He had been teaching them for three years. Incredibly refined boys both, he recalled. It had been a pleasure to sit in front of that grand beauty in the middle of the hall overlooking the sea. The parents had not known how to tell him to stop coming to the house. It must have been a relief for them when the boys decided to go overseas for higher studies.

A blustering wind swept the curtain, and toppled the candle-stand that stood on the piano. Batliboi straggled to pick it up. Musty smell of wood turned damp; a dampness seeping in from the walls and the ceiling. He must get the piano away from the wall. He got his grip on the edge of the old piece and pushed. Pushed hard. His whole body shuddered against the solid wood. Not an inch, it did not move. Tremulous hands placed the candles back in the wrought iron candle-stand. For a long time after that Batliboi stood looking at them. Percy! How he remembered her....

The little girl from Bandra; eleven years old, she'd wait for him every evening, her manuscript book on her lap, sitting outside in the balcony, so she could play for him what he'd taught her the day before. He had learnt to love her dearly. She had set her heart on music. 'One day I'm going to be a great pianist', she would tell him. That's all she ever wanted from life. Music! Music! Music! In the summer of 1986 she'd started to feel tired for no obvious reason. Her nerves had frayed, leaving her enervated most of the time and before anyone realised it, she was in the hospital, diagnosed with a disease that was fatal. The music had died out. Percy was in the last stage of her illness. That whole summer he tried to go see her. Perhaps he could play for her; it would cheer her a bit. One day as he landed at the building in Khar Danda road, he saw the piano being carried out.

'For money,' said the family.

'There isn't enough money for my treatment!' Percy had told him, her eyes glistening.

'But music could give her life,' he'd argued with her parents.

'She can either get medicine or play the piano for a few more weeks...,' was what they'd said.

Percy hadn't looked at him all afternoon as he sat by her bedside. She'd kept staring at the candle-stand that used to stand on the piano, now placed on the mantlepiece across her bed next to the picture of Jesus, the Saviour.

'I want you to keep it. For me.' She'd smiled, four white candles shining in her moist eyes.

Three months after the piano was sold, Percy died in hospital.

It must have been right after that, that the hands began to tremble, thought Batliboi. He tried to hold a key down. A hollow nothingness emanated from it; a dull ache of soundlessness. He hadn't touched these keys in months now. The piano was out of tune. He beat the key down with all his strength, his scanty white hair falling around his bony face in dishevelled strands. He hit the key again! And again! And again! The notes scuttled across the room, corner to corner, through the ceiling, against the damp walls and back.

Batliboi stood stooped over the piano, his limbs fraught with inadequacy. Why won't the keys be still? Why did these hands tremble...oh damn! The ultimate music! To attain that final silence of a note. A maverick wind swept moist his face. The windowpane dashed against the ledge. Batliboi lifted his hands up to his face, scrawny fingers trembling against an overcast sky.

'Another man's wife...she was...another man's...,' he mumbled across the room.

His left foot tripped over the Iranian rug, where it had worn down to a sieve. A grey star in a dark blue floor-sky. He regained balance. The phone bill had to be paid or else the line would get disconnected. And then, no one will ever be able to call him to come tune a piano. He scrambled through the leather diary again, the one that was frayed, its crimson turned to brown. There was no pension for a pianist and there had never been any savings. He wouldn't dare touch the fixed deposit. That was the only thing that had kept him going all these years. I will call that...that actress who lived in Juhu. But Juhu was at the other end of Bombay city. So what, he checked himself. He'd take the Borivali fast train and get off at

Andheri. From there he could always take an autorickshaw; won't cost much.

She was the quiet, sensitive type...'artistic,' he'd been told last year when he met her. He hadn't noticed her demeanour. He remembered walking onto a terrace instead of a sitting room. There, across the floor of an open kitchen, was the black upright piano holding burnt sunflowers in a tall glass jar. He had touched it at once to feel the wood.

'I painted it black,' she spoke softly. 'I paint....'

He had pulled out the stool and sat down to open the lid, dislodging the green velvet cloth that covered the well-dusted keyboard. The white keys emerged like a smile.

'A piano should never be kept out on the terrace. You'll ruin it,' he'd spoken, looking down, fiddling with the keys. 'The breeze will eat it up!'

He almost hadn't noticed her standing in the corner looking at him with curiosity. A study! He must be a study for her, a character. At that instant, he remembered now, how acutely aware he had become of the enormity of his nose, the uneasy proportion of his legs, the knees jutting out, like fists, the dome of his back and the trembling...of his hands.

'It doesn't belong to me,' she said, 'I don't know how to look after it. A friend left it here when she moved to America. *She* was an *ace* pianist!'

The words did not jam into each other like *an eggbeater pressed down*. There were spaces, silent ones, for each word to linger and float...acquire a rhythm of its own.

Feroze Batliboi looked up. 'Do you play it?' Yes, she *was* studying him, he could tell from her expression.

'I'd love to. I love music. I do play it. Not like piano though! Like...like wind...like clouds...unstructured...unstudied... unlearnt....' And then she smiled. Batliboi relaxed. He played a few keys as though everything was okay with his hands. But his head, never theless, shook.

'Would you like to learn?'

'No…not really…not in that sense…not from the book…there are keys here that won't make a sound.'

She suddenly bent down to touch three chords. 'I want you to bring them back to life. Can you?'

Batliboi looked up. He saw her eyes move in concomitance with the shaking of his head.

Yes, yes, she's the one. He would call her. Right away. Should have thought of her in the first place. How did he forget? He had even bought those three wires he'd been meaning to change for her. They must be in this lower drawer somewhere.

Bent over the Chinese cabinet, Batliboi rummaged through old cuttings, scores, printed manuscripts, loose notation sheets, flinging the chords around in the air…until he could feel in his hands the brown paper bag. Three coiled wires glistened on his palm, the quivering intensifying the shimmer. He pulled out an old watch from his pocket. Five-thirty in the morning. It was still dark outside, too early to call anyone. He snapped the watch close and scrambled the chain back into the fob. He would have to wait.

The dark clouds drifted and floated across to the far end of the sea. Lights still glimmered in the city skyline, now hazier with mist. He opened the cupboard, once again tripping on the star sliver in the night blue rug. A face in the mirror swung back and forth like a pendulum. He pulled out his grey jacket. He always wore it over his khaki trousers. He needed to wear a tie, or perhaps not. In Bombay, it was only the monsoon months that had some semblance to a winter. Jerky hands shuffled a tie into a knot. He felt the inside of his coat pocket to make sure he was carrying the chords with him.

He reached for a washcloth and wiped the Hush Puppies brown. His hair, he left like that.

The scent of the monsoon in his veins, Batliboi stood at the window once again looking at the lights on the streets, forever moving, forever changing. The deluge had begun to ebb away. The din of the city had receded to the sea.

Piano-forte: a large musical instrument played by pressing the black or the white keys of the keyboard (1b), thus causing small hammers to strike metal strings to produce different notes. He remembered his father teaching him.

One finger at a time first, then all five and both hands. Crotchets...quavers...semi quavers...to hit a key and suddenly lift off the hand. It's called staccato! Staccato! He'd loved the word then, he loved it, still.

A round stool swirled. Thin strands of white hair framed a lifetime of solitude. A nose stood distinguished, apart. Stooping, stumping over keys, the blacks and the whites alternately caving in, Feroze Batliboi sat down at his piano and started to play.

Across the room a woman sat looking at him, mesmerised.

He would play tonight; music for the sake of music...melody for the sake of melody...no matter how his hands quivered! No matter how the notes strayed!

Nothing structured, nothing studied, he would...unlearn...he would unlearn....

He would play with the wind...with the clouds.... He would bring back to life...the notes that had died....

He would play for himself...melodies old and precious.

And he would play for *her*...the woman sitting across the room,
looking at him with sad, wanting eyes.

❦

 Sisters

Blue linen scarves wrapped around their heads, the sisters from Joginder Nagar walked through the main bazaar, one step at a time, their heads hanging low. Little street boys ran behind them, pulling at their scarves to reveal their shaven heads. Street vendors shoved their carts into corners at the turning to let the girls pass by. Shopkeepers stood at their thresholds to witness the sight.

Bunny, thirteen, and Ginny, twelve, dressed for some godforsaken reason, in long kameezes with knickers underneath, looked more like children out of a prison cell rather than two young girls out of a barbershop in a quaint north Indian hill town. The only sign of femininity visible on them was the silver anklets they wore, one each on their bare feet.

Peals of laughter followed them around the corner where the main street branched off into a gully. A boy in scraggly half pants selling bangles and *parandis,* chased the girls all the way to the bus stop, mock-pleading with them to buy the long thread braids with gold tassles hanging at the ends. Bunny and Ginny ducked for shelter. Teasingly he dangled the black braids in front of them, shedding gold dust in their faces, creating a tamasha for all to see.

It was no secret in town that the much-respected Bada Saab of Badi Kothi, the handsome Bau Balram Chand, had turned into a total waste after his wife had left him. The couple, Balram and Tara, and their much envied love marriage, once the talk of the small town had quickly sunk into acrimony. The man had become a complete alcoholic. In fact, he had been of late, so gone, that he had been found on several occasions, in a complete state of disarray; half slumped in the gutter by the toe-path along the slope of the hill that led to the Badi Kothi, the only large mansion in the district that stood regally aloof, unfrequented and reeking of decadence, overlooking the small railway track that ran through the valley.

By now everyone in the little town knew about the plight of the sisters. Mother having gone away, and the girls left at the mercy of a distant aunt or worse still, under the care of an alcoholic father, whom ironically, they had to take turns tending to, rather than it being the other way around.

Balram Chand had lost the will to go on without his wife, whom he had been unable to go on *with*, any longer. To gather himself and rise to the occasion; to be able to provide for, and to protect his daughters was a task he found himself incapable of handling, leave alone being able to handle two beautiful young girls with long lustrous hair infested with lice!

The lice had started to breed and proliferate causing reddish abrasions on their scalps. No amount of combing helped. Neither was of any use the nightly oiling of their hair, repeated applications of the lice medicine: white powder mixed with mustard oil, out of the brown glass bottle, and tying up the long tresses in white cotton cloth, to be kept overnight for best results.

Ginny, on her side of the bed, would lie awake scratching her head through the muslin wrap, and Bunny, unable to bear the itching any longer, would end up throwing away the soiled wrap and using both her hands scratch herself to sleep again.

A maid was brought in. Just to tackle the lice situation. But despite combing the long strands endlessly with the finest of combs meant to dredge the lice out, she achieved little result. The wounds would rake up every time the girls scratched their scalps with their nails. So bad was the condition that the sisters, finally, out of embarrassment, stopped going to school and stayed back home most part of their day, scratching. The itching and scratching had caused deep calluses and the wounds, so severe, had begun to ooze.

'Cut it off!' Bau Balram Chand had insouciantly ordered Nai, the local barber who had been called in, as the girls stood in the pillared verandah, petrified at the prospect of a life, thereafter.

The last time he had been called in at the Badi Kothi was when the sisters were toddlers, due for their mundan ceremony.

'No, but...,' the girls stuttered.

'No *buts*!' roared Balram Chand. 'Cut it all off! Shave off their heads!'

Long, silky strands of luscious, black hair fell to the floor where Bunny and Ginny sat teary-eyed in front of the mirror at the only local male barbershop in town.

The sisters had fought hard to protect their vanity, but no amount of crying or pleading was to prevent the galling incident that happened in Joginder Nagar, one late afternoon, back in the 1960s.

Ginny clung onto the arm of the chair, fidgeting violently, stamping her feet on the floor. Bunny shrieked and kicked, her long pink-ribboned braids slapping about her. Nai, gaunt and square-faced, stood behind them with a pair of scissors in his hand. The mirror reflected a knot of faces peering at them through the glass pane; little street boys glued to the window, mesmerised by this rare, strange sight: two girls getting their long hair chopped.

The girls had somehow managed to convince Nai to give them, not a shave, but a close crop — a boy cut!

One look at the girls standing in the courtyard of the house — their hair cropped and Bryl-creamed — looking more like wet crows and Bau Balram Chand, in his drunken stupor, roared indignantly:

19

'CUT IT ALL OFF, I said, Didn't I? SHAVE OFF THEIR HEADS!'

Back to the barbershop the girls were sent. This time round, no screaming; it was a wordless revolt, not so silent though. A shuffling of feet, a tearing of hands, unclenching of fists, flailing of arms and the back and forth dragging of chairs. Ginny held onto the arm of the chair, refusing to be clambered back into it one more time. Bunny knew better. She held her cropped head in both her hands and ducked to her knees, and when nothing else worked, she finally swooped down to the floor, thrashing about her limbs, in muffled retaliation.

All of this, while Nai stood quietly behind them, this time holding in his hands not scissors but an *ustara*, a metal razor — the kind they used for prisoners in the local cell in Kangra jail — waiting patiently for the girls to succumb to their fate.

'Just a few nicks and cuts! That's all!' he said, his eyes pleading, guilty.

The old chap couldn't have found a worse way of putting it. Might as well, as unwittingly, he'd put it, the way it was to be.

A few *nicks and cuts* at the self-esteem of two pretty little pahari girls growing up in a place like this....

The machinery was set to work; the undoing of what could have been a beautiful adolescence had begun. The girls shut their eyes tight as they sat cowering in their chairs, hissing with silent rage.

A rapid grazing of the scalp, the rhythmic *khach* — *khach* — *khach* — *khach* — *khach* of the shaving machine, the raw metal dodging scabs; chafing sensitive skin. When Nai was finally done with the sisters, two perfectly round, pink heads emerged bewildered in the barber's rust-flecked mirror.

Such disgrace!

Bunny and Ginny held their heads in shame. One step at a time, the entire length of the bazaar they walked once again, their eyes glued to the ground below their feet.

A fat boy on a bicycle came riding straight towards them. The sisters knew him. He was this cheeky fellow, son of the munshi, who would come prying into the Kothi along with his father when books of accounts were being revised, and each time Tara would make him sit on the bench outside, he would wince. But today was his day! Bunny held on tightly to Ginny's hand. The girls scurried to the corner of the street and stood on the wooden plank above the *naali*, holding tightly onto each other.

The grinning boy rode straight on and tugged at Ginny's scarf. The girl lost her balance and stumbled over the loose brick threshold and fell to the ground. The fat boy's cycle jammed into the *phatta* above the *naali* and toppled. Bunny shut her eyes and squeezed herself into the wall. The boy skidded over to the other side of the narrow street. Ginny looked up through the spinning wheel of the toppled bicycle, her bald scalp shimmering in the sun.

Bunny extended her hand, helping her sister back on her feet. In doing so her own scarf slipped and fell. A fresh peal of laughter rippled about them. Ginny scrambled back onto her feet, quickly shuffling the muslin back in place. Then holding onto each other again, the sisters turned into the toe-path going downhill and hurried towards home.

Once inside the main gate of the Kothi, the girls broke down in loud sobs.

How could a father put his daughters to such shame! Such humiliation! It was all their mother's fault! Why had she gone away to Nani's house? Why had she left? Had she been here this would *never* have happened! How could she have done this? Leave the house! Leave her daughters at the mercy of their drunkard father! How would *he ever* know what it felt like to have their long beautiful hair cut off? Chopped! Shaven! Made bald? Were they to be punished for their beauty?

That night the girls swore they would never speak to Mummy again.

21

Evening had set in quietly. A cool wind was starting up.

Ginny stood at the mantlepiece, chipping into the yellowed white wall, scratching with her thumb nail, the loose damp paint cakes, powder-flaking to the floor. Bunny sat by the wooden threshold of the hall, staring at the sparklers that rose in the still-smouldering fireplace. Somewhere in the house an open windowpane banged relentlessly with the wind.

Pretty girls, they say, don't grow up on remote hillsides without having their fathers go insane. More than the aspect of having to deal with lice, it was the sudden turning of male heads in the bazaar that was driving Bau Balram Chand paranoid each time he walked with his girls through the old market place.

Sitting in his wicker chair, Balram Chand did not look out at the path that led up to the Badi Kothi. He'd been puking all evening and had not made even a slight gesture of regret or remorse towards his daughters for what he had done to them. That both the girls had taken silent turns in cleaning up the spew around him all evening, was something he would not be aware of.

It was on nights like this, when the train glided in silently making only smoke sounds that the sisters ever let the idea of running away from home, encroach their minds. To entertain such an idea would be blasphemous and had to undoubtedly be driven out of their little heads.

The train passing by the valley whistled low that night, a hollow, apprehensive whistle. From the verandah, where the sisters sat defiant, they could see, down below in the valley, the railway track of Joginder Nagar, the last station on the Kangra Junction. It was sparingly lit, the platform. The last passenger train was seen pulling out. There was one more to go that night. The goods-rail; it left at 10.20.

The sisters did not exchange a glance. Each stood her ground, ensconced in her own thoughts, taking stock of the unusual happenings in remote hill towns. That their thoughts had been uncannily similar that night was revealed only once the clock sounded the hour ten. In the next twenty minutes the last goods train would leave the station.

A train whistle reverberated through the valley like a siren. Slowly and simultaneously the sisters turned their heads to gauge each other.

A cold, hard wind whipped the broken bay windows of the Kothi.

A season changed.

Skidding downhill at great speed, two pairs of feet hurtled rapidly down the slope, the silver anklets jingling, squelching through puddles, grazing wet, wild grass and rushes.

If Balram Chand had not been so drunk that night, he would have, from his window, seen his girls running away from a life they could no longer fathom living.

The lights from distant houses flashed dizzily past as the girls took long strides into the dark night, running, falling, getting up and running again, their hands clasped together, barefoot through shrubs and bushes, down, down to the railway track, in a desperate attempt to grab the only chance they had of getting away from their wretched existence, their freshly shaved heads stinging with the first wintry wind.

Black crows on barbed wires fled into the darkness flapping their wings, making startling night sounds. It was the last goods train, signalling its departure; they had to catch it!

Ducking under barbed wires, they jumped the animal fence and leapt towards the railway track. This was the third and final whistle. It was only four minutes to go, when panting, and out of breath, the sisters made it to the gravel, skipping on sleeperwood slats a little short of the main platform.

Heavy wheels of steel squeaked on metallic tracks. Bunny shot a desperate glance towards Ginny.

Freedom! Freedom was here at last!

Just one more leap! Freedom from the drilling night sounds of their parents, fighting constantly till the wee hours of the morning; freedom from having to mother an alcoholic father, forever in a state of inebriation; freedom from the paranoia of a mother behind closed doors, endlessly washing and re-washing her hands at the sink, an act that was suspected to have driven Bau Balram Chand to the bottle, or whichever way around that may have been!

But *freedom*!

Standing out there in sweat and cold, the sisters exchanged frightened, urgent glances, then looked all around.

'There is no one...let's go!' Bunny darted towards the train. Only three minutes left.

Then, she stopped.

'Wait! How can we do this? How can we go? Run away from home...and go...where? Leave father all alone! Who will look after him? How will he survive...without mother first, and now, without us?'

But no! There was no time for guilt!

The goods train that had shuffled into position, stood hissing, waiting for two young girls to make a decision, a life-altering decision. But what do you expect from girls, barely twelve and thirteen, faced with such predicaments?

Bunny and Ginny looked at each other with urgency. There was no time to think. There was just this one moment. A decision had to be made. It was now or never.

Bunny lunged towards the bogey. A silver anklet jingled on the edge of the red metal threshold. A hand clutched the iron bar. She shot a glance back at her sister and held her hand out.

'Ginny! Come...!'

A whistle blew. A heavy metal lever ratcheted and fell back in place. The light on the signal changed from red to green. The flagman at the other end of the platform rolled up the red cloth and let the green flag in his hand fall, waving it up and down, indicating —

All clear! All clear to go!

The train hissed for a bit as if waiting still, for the girls to make up their minds, then, slowly, started to trundle out.

'Ginny!...run...!'

Ginny suddenly stood on the platform, dazed.

'I...I...can't...,' she stuttered, her voice weak as a whisper.

Bunny stepped off the bogey and started to walk alongside the train, her one hand still clutching the metal bar.

'Ginny, come!...there's still time! Come! We can get away!'

Bunny's throat was choked with a voice Ginny hadn't heard before. Her eyes were blaring with a desire for another world. But the younger one stood motionless on the platform. The train slowly started to speed up. Bunny was now running alongside it, her hand still held out, her voice, fraught with frenzy.

'Ginny! RUN!...It's *NOW OR NEVER!*'

But the expression on her sister's face told her it was going to be *never*.

Ginny's feet trailed reluctantly on the gravel, her eyes welling up with tears. She was now skidding behind Bunny, unable to say what she felt in her heart. Then, in a frenetic moment, her voice choking with another kind of emotion, tearfully she shrieked,

'What if MUMMY CAME BACK?'

Bunny's hand let go of the metal bar. A cold wind stung her scalp where the metal razor had grazed the skin. Startled into reality, she slowly came and stood before her younger sister, the last goods train fleeting past behind; in her ears, train sounds colliding.

Breathless stood the sisters, looking at each other, crestfallen, flashes of light slicing rapidly their gaunt, stunned faces.

A decision had been taken.

The shift changed. At the far end of the platform the old flagman checked the metre in the cabin and locked up for the night. From where he stood, he looked at the railway track for any signs of movement. The train receding in the distance was now reduced to a speck in the landscape. A train whistle reverberated through the valley of Joginder Nagar and died out. All was well.

Then his eyes fell upon the gravelled, far end of the platform.

Under the lamppost, huddled on a bench, two bald heads shone dimly in the foggy night.

 Premonition

Vas, tall, dark, lean, and all of nineteen, shuffled his backpack onto the overhead rack and carefully pressed himself into the dark green rexine covered seat. The bus was more than two hours late and he was thankful to have finally got on. Passengers moved back and forth; bottles of water and other refreshments passed through the barred windows. People jostled, tickets in hand, ducking to read the numbers on the sides of the seats; a bit of musical chairs, and then finally everyone settled in. The bus driver hopped sprightly onto his seat, the conductor blew the whistle and the bus was all set to pull out of the main Dadar bus terminal. It was going to be a long ride back to Bangalore. Vas felt lucky to have found a window seat.

This was his first trip ever to Bombay. He had come to the city to meet his friend who was now settled here. Fact was, he had been called in to meet the friend's girlfriend, whom he had decided to get married to. Vas was the chosen *close one* to meet the girl and give a final approval. He had liked the girl instantly and even felt amused giving his blessings, as do in-laws. He was happy that his friend had found a great girl and after spending an exultant week in the metropolis it was now time to get back home. Vas felt elated.

It was about six-thirty and the hills around Khandala Ghat looked enchanting in the evening light. Vas stuck his head out a bit to let the cool breeze graze his face. He sat gazing at the landscape just outside of Panvel as trees, fields, huts all flashed past in rapid, dry brush strokes. He then put his head back on the headrest and started to dream…his dream of meeting a nice girl himself, someday: a girl who would make his head turn.

Vas felt the first flutter of discomfort in his gut when, in the middle of the animated conversation between the driver and the conductor, the bus leaped into the air, and with a jolt, fell back on the tarred road, sending a small boulder hurtling down the edge of the precipice. Vas's head nearly hit the luggage rack above. His backpack fell on him. Oops! The two men burst out laughing. Vas wasn't sure if he liked that kind of humour. He clutched his onto backpack tightly in his arms, shifted in his seat to reaffirm his position of comfort, then went back to snoozing again.

Suddenly, he felt strange. The bus was driving close to the edge of the road. Looking down at the sheer drop, he was saying to himself, I'm not scared of heights! Yet, illogically, in the pit of his stomach, something started to unsettle. What if there was an accident?

The thought, once planted, started to build up in his head. It was something like a premonition. Vas sat back in his seat, alert, circumspect, his back taut with both fear and apprehension…. No, it was more fear he felt…fear that something terrible was going to happen.

Vas rose from his seat, then, again sat down. He shuffled his knees, crossing one leg to the other, then, reverting to the way it was. He looked around. Everyone seemed to be enjoying the ride through the sun-spilled ghats. He apparently was the only one scared. He turned his head to look back. One seat behind him, sitting next to an old man, was a young woman, looking at him. Vas straightened up. There was something striking about her. Slowly he turned back again, caught her eye. Yes, she *was* looking at him: a dark, attractive woman with large, luminous, kajal-lined eyes!

A woman who had made his head turn!

Vas at once became self-conscious; the blood in his veins, surging. There was, on an overnight bus to Bangalore, a woman, very beautiful, *looking at him*! Stealthily, he turned and looked at her face. He assumed she would be about twenty-five; older woman. But what the heck! She looked stunning in a night blue sari with a white woven border. Vas was not one to let these little details escape him. And in her nose she wore a dazzling nose ring that enhanced her immaculate bone-structure.

He shifted in his seat to re-adjust his position, sitting on a slant, half front, and half facing the dark beauty. And now he started eyeballing her, a mysterious little game to keep his mind off the *fear*. He would glance at her, their eyes would meet, and she would quickly look away, a perfectly chiselled, amber profile sunlit against the glass window. The rhythmic swaying of the bus, her jhumkas tinkling, the shy, stolen glances; Vas was enraptured.

Soon the sun went down. Vas started to get the same sinking feeling again. Each time the bus jerked or another horn blared in his ears, he felt ridiculously stupid for jumping out of his seat! Worse, he was sure the woman could tell he was scared.

Sounds shifted. The sense of evening passed away and night fell around him in a strange way, alienating Vas from the landscape he was journeying through. The sky outside the window was now pitch dark and the lights in the bus had been switched off.

Vas couldn't keep looking back any longer. No matter how much he craned his neck to get a glance of the woman, her face was now decidedly in the dark. The only glimpse he got of her was, when a passing vehicle flashed its light on the glass window, and that light reflected on her face.

So each time a car or a lorry headed towards the bus from the opposite direction, Vas would get ready to catch her face in the passing light. He learnt to time the passing of vehicles in a manner that as they zipped by, he'd swiftly turn his head around to get a fleeting glimpse of the dark beauty.

This woman would be…what, five to six years older than him, Vas was thinking. Not too much of a chance…but let me try at least, being friends with her! After all, he did find himself drawn to older women!

A vehicle would zip past, the glass window would glint, Vas would shoot a glance back, and for one mercurial moment, the woman's face would light up!

The woman soon caught onto this little game, but what she did not fathom was that for Vas it was not a frivolous thing. Her presence somehow assuaged his fear of the premonition; fear that something terrible was going to happen to the bus. If he did not do that, did not distract himself by playing with her, he'd be petrified of the *accident*. It was so bizarre!

It was nearly ten in the night. Everyone around had started to doze, but for Vas. His eyes were clear, sleepless. He peered intensely into the charcoal night. He noticed that the woman too had started to doze off. He was the only one wide awake.

Finally the bus slowed down to halt for a dinner break. It was a chai ka dhaaba, a rickety old place. People shuffled in their seats. Vas felt it was time he spoke to the woman. He waited in his seat while other people disembarked. But she was busy tending to the old man sitting with her. She helped him off the bus, walked him to the men's makeshift toilet, walked back and tucked him in his seat. Then, to Vas's great excitement, she started to move towards the exit again. He quickly followed. As she got off this time, Vas made direct eye contact with her.

'Is everything alright with the old uncle?' Vas asked with a great amount of familiarity.

The woman paused for a bit, looking at Vas. He could not gauge what her reaction at that moment would be.

'Where are you from?'

He tried to go on with something like a conversation. The young woman looked around towards where the old man sat, then, turning back to Vas, whispered in Kannada, '*Aameley*!'

Later, she implied, with a movement of her hand.

Vas was thrilled. That was all he needed to hear. *Later*. As she gesticulated, Vas had noticed that the young woman was holding a book in her hand, a book by the Kannada writer, U.R. Ananthamurthy, Vas's favourite writer. That immediately for him, was a rush. Something called *connect* happened that very instant! There was hope for Vas. She is no bimbette, he thought. She is beautiful, and then, bright enough to be reading a highly acclaimed writer...he has a chance!

The young man who returned to his dark green window seat was one assured of his charms. She had said, *later*, so he was going to wait. For later. Vas closed his eyes.

It must have been around midnight. Vas had just about managed to fall asleep when a nasty bump suddenly bounced him awake. He felt sick with a giddy-in-the-head kind of feeling. His bladder felt really full. The fear was worsening his urge to pee. Vas looked around. Most of the passengers were sleeping; their bodies limply swaying to the curves and ditches on the un-tarred bifurcation of the main highway. Vas turned his head. The woman and the old man, both were asleep. He walked to the front of the bus and stood with a look of urgency on his face, waiting for the driver to notice him. When the man finally looked up, Vas held out his little finger, pointing upward.

'Wait,' said the conductor, 'till next stop.'

Vas glared at the man, squeezing his knees together, a glint building in his eyes.

'Return fast, *hanh*! *Jaldi aana*! We're running late!' the driver reluctantly pressed his foot on the break.

Vas rushed out and scrambled about near the trees to take a leak Aaah! What relief! He looked up at the stars in the night sky; felt the cool breeze permeate every pore of his body. Peeing was such bliss, such bliss!

'Pom! Pom! Pom!'

The driver was honking wildly. Vas struggled with his zipper and quickly got back onto the bus. In five minutes he started to berate himself for being so foolish and superstitious. I understand science, he argued with himself. Not much of a believer in God and all that, but I'm a fairly rational kind of a guy! What is wrong with me? The bus is fine. It's just an illogical fear I'm suffering from…that the bus is going to crash! Rubbish!

Vas tried to get his mind off the madness that was fast threatening to engulf him. How could he think like that? It was crazy! See, how people around were so trustfully sleeping in their seats? No one seemed to be even remotely bothered about the way the bus was going or where it was going. Vas curled up his jacket to fit it in the crook of his neck, using it as a pillow. He tilted his head to rest against the window and shut his eyes. He must get sleep. He must. The metallic drone of the engine was constant. Soon his head rolled back and forth with the rhythmic jerks.

Slowly sounds began to transform into shapes; the shape of things; was it shadows or figures…it was something else…like liquid…floating, oily dark liquid, thick, un-swallowable! A dense black liquid streaked with grey, rapidly flowing past. Vas's head flowed with it, or floated…it was unclear. A flash of light now and then came through the darkness. Then several flashes, breaking up the liquid flow, like effects created on the stage for the play he had designed in college. But it wasn't the same. Somehow this light was threatening; it flashed menacingly through the black fluid.

The first tingling of wetness around his temples started. His grip on his backpack tightened. Vas was trying hard to fight the shapes unfurling in his head. His toes curled up inside his shoes. His neck felt stiff and hard. His eyes shut tight.

Then Vas recognised it. It was a floodlight flashing from the opposite direction. It came closer and closer at great speed, and then, then the moment just stretched…. Vas sees the bus go off the road…a large leap into the air…and slowly it turns on itself and...begins to fall...rolling over in mid air...plunging into the deep gorge! It continues to fall...a great fall....

Beads of sweat erupted on Vas's face. His skin tingled with it, glistening in the sick smell. Yes, he could see it coming, the crash! A head-on collision! A fall, a great fall! He knew it was going to happen! He had a premonition!

Vas suddenly sat up in his seat, breathless; desperate now to make friends with the young woman. I am going to talk to her for sure, he decided.

This driver is drunk! He doesn't know how to drive! He is going to kill us all! Shit man! This is no good! I don't want to be on this bus! I'm getting off! This bus has to be stopped. It *must* be stopped. This accident has to be stopped from happening! But no one seemed too bothered or aware of the ghastly calamity that awaited them around the next corner. Fools! Fools they were, all of them, sleeping. But he was not to be one of them. No! He was not going any further on this bus! Not on this bus! He was going to get out! Save his life! He was not going to die out here! He was not going to die!

Vas sat up with a jolt, shaking. In a desperate attempt, he turned his head to look at the woman, hoping she'd be awake. Accidently at a bump, she'd sort of, semi-wake up and give him a check. Vas desperately needed that one acknowledgement from her, Look! I'm still here...still looking at you!

Suddenly the woman turned, and opened those large, sleepy eyes. Now when the whole bus was asleep, the young woman actually smiled at him. The look on her face: Oh my god! You are awake, and *still* looking at me!

In the next hour or so it started to rain. And she quickly dozed off again, setting into a deep slumber. All seemed still and well.

Finally at some point, late in the night, the bus stopped. Vas heard the conductor wake up and announce the name of a small village that had come up. The man sitting next to Vas moved in his seat. This was his chance. He would get off right now and get the hell out of here. There was no point in trying to save the lives of all these other people; no one would believe that he had this premonition; that he *knew* what was going to happen! To tell them to get off the bus because they were all going to die would be futile. They would laugh at him.

Vas grabbed his meagre belongings, and scurried towards the front exit. The driver looked up. Vas quickly looked away as if trying to hide his guilt; guilt for deserting all these people, leaving them to die. At the exit Vas stopped. How could he? *She* was on the bus too!

To his utter surprise, amongst a few other passengers alighting the bus in this godforsaken place, was also the young woman with the old man, pushing towards the exit. They too were getting off! What? Here? In the middle of nowhere? As the woman passed him, Vas, in his eyes, had many questions.

'Shimoga,' she said gently. 'From here we are taking a bus to Shimoga.' And followed the old man, ushering him towards the front exit.

Shimoga? She is going to Shimoga? At that instance Vas took an impulsive decision. This is my chance. I am getting off this bus and going with *her*! To Shimoga! There were two other people who got off the bus behind him. 'Lucky guys, got saved!' he mumbled to himself as he toe-trailed the woman in the dark.

'That was close!' he gasped, scrambling into the next bus after her.

This time he made sure he sat close to her. He didn't think twice before rudely nudging the fat lady aside and squeezing himself into the seat right behind the young woman.

Whatever the place, wherever they were heading, Vas first got in after this woman, only then did he start thinking. This place should be somewhere on the border between Maharashtra and Karnataka. So this was in the general direction towards Karnataka. This woman was obviously not from Bangalore city; she was taking a detour. The only bell Shimoga rang in his head was, all pretty, intelligent girls came from either Malnad or from Shimoga!

As the bus pulled out in the dark, a yellow street-lamp brought into light, a black & white signboard that read, Chitradurga. As all this was unplanned, Vas jingled together whatever money he had in his wallet and made sure there was enough for the detour. Was it one or one-thirty in the night, he could not figure out; his sense of space and time that night was completely warped.

Once Vas had decidedly settled in, the old uncle turned back to look at him, giving him an unapproving glare. He'd probably caught on that the youngster was hitting upon his niece. Vas keenly watched the old man's profile with intent. He could've been her grandfather or uncle or something; he seemed about sixty-ish.

Vas could now look at his ladylove in minute detail: her hair, her shoulder, her neck, her jhumkas jingling away with the rhythm of the bus. The dark dusky beauty had a lovely six-stone nose stud, typically South Indian. He could only see her right earring; the left one was pressed against the window. Carefully and strategically he placed his hand behind her neck with the excuse of holding the steel bar. His fingers were so close to her skin; if the bus swayed, his left hand on the rod would touch the nape of her neck. That was electric! Almost like erotic tension; it was beautiful!

Vas was now seeking an opportunity to speak to her. But she did not once turn around to make eye contact. Vas, nevertheless, felt super fine! He was on another bus; that ominous bus was gone. His fear psychosis had come to rest.

The woman was quite amused with this up-close and personal scrutinising that was going on from one seat behind. Yes she was nervous; the old man had caught on to it, yet, she felt flattered, also surprised. She could not determine whether the youngster was simply trailing her, stringing along for kicks, or whether he was genuinely going that same route.

Sometime along the night, the old man dozed off. That's when the woman turned softly, and without words, with just her eyes, smiled.

This, for Vas, was heavenly! It meant promise!

So what if she is older! He argued still with himself. Come on, what has age got to do with all this? It's bullshit, this thing about age! Vas also noticed that she was not wearing a taali, the mangal-sutra. Till then, he hadn't been smart enough to think whether the woman was married or not. So the absence of the taali was a thing of beauty, a thrill. Okay, at least she is single!

Gradually they both dozed off. But once in a while, in that half sleep, that dream-like state, he'd wake up or she'd wake up and they would both vaguely acknowledge each other. It was a very dreamy, quixotic state. It was like slipping into a dream, coming back, slipping into dream again.... The next few hours of sleeping, not sleeping, the pleasure, the thrill of anticipation, and for Vas, the excitement of waking up in the morning and getting to know what her name was.

The sky was beginning to lighten at the edges; a pinkish hue that signals the night is going to be over. Vas opened his eyes and stretched his arms a bit. His back hurt from slouching in his seat through the long night. A hazy greenish tint filled the winter landscape. No, it was not day as yet, but was about to be. Birds, breeze, and faint and distant, the sound of a horn; a bus! Slowly the ambiguous, dense grey fields started to come alive. An orange light was emerging on the horizon...day was breaking....

As the bus turned from the dust track and got on to the tarred road towards the bridge, Vas saw in the semi-darkness of daybreak, birds migrating. He saw the river like he'd never seen it before. He hadn't even noticed the sky as much, ever. He craned his neck to look at the water as the bus approached the bridge.

But as the bus neared the bridge, Vas saw a steel rod give way.... He gasped, wanted to shout but no voice came out of his throat.

Then he saw a pillar slip under the bridge and bricks sprouting out. Vas ran towards the driver, shouting, without voice! And then the moment stretches.... Vas sees in exhaustive detail: the bus steer right off the bridge...a long leap in the air...and slowly turns on itself, and begins to tumble...rolling over in the air...plunging into the gravelled slope...it continues to fall...a great fall....

'Brake! Brake! Brake!'

Vas could hear voices now, people screaming. It was a stunning moment for him to realise this was no nightmare! This was real! It was really happening! At that instant when the bus steered off the road and plumetted into the gorge, he heard words:

'*Roko!*' '*Roko!*' 'Control it!' 'Turn it this side!' 'No!' Shouting!

Vas could see everything with great clarity. But it was numbing, the feeling.... Things were happening too quickly. The bus overturned. That's when it all became very confusing. When the bus toppled, when it literally fell upside down, it was completely disorienting.

Vas didn't know what way what was. He just tried to hold onto whatever he could. His body was tossed and he hit the roof. In exhaustive detail he saw the world tousle before his eyes. Suddenly the seats were above him. He was stuck with some bags and some people had fallen over him.

And then there was half an eerie silence, people panicking, some crying, some people moaning, and the bus was shaking still. Some broken glass sounds; things still falling slowly; people trying to get up, struggling, just enough light to discern shapes and bearings.

Vas squeezed himself through the smashed glass of a broken window. As he crawled out, in his left shoulder he felt a shooting pain! There were a few passersby, villagers and farmers, some four or five people. They were extricating people, pulling them out, helping whomever they could.

Only when Vas crawled out, did he realise how fatal this accident could have been. Wheels were upturned. Some people were bleeding, some crying; a farmer helped Vas onto his feet. Once he saw that he was okay, the man rushed back to help others. For Vas, it took him a minute or two to realise that he had survived. He saw the driver being pulled out, either unconscious or dead; he was bleeding profusely. Vas wasn't bleeding but his left shoulder.... Then he felt something like relief!

My god! This is what I was afraid would happen, and it *has* happened! My premonition *has* come true! This is it! The worst is over! I have survived! I am alive!

For those few minutes Vas forgot all about the woman. The shock, the excruciating shoulder pain, the psychological relief; it took him a while before the thought came to his mind:

Oh, the woman! What happened to *her*?

Clutching his throbbing shoulder he started to move closer to the bus. He tried to see in the semi-darkness of the morning and the confusion. Could he spot the woman? Where was she? Where was the old man?

Now he saw from the tang bund; there was the road, and below, was the lake. The road was thirty feet higher. Vehicles were stopping up there now and people were running down to come and see what had happened. The traffic was beginning to pile up. A few buses, some lorries, villagers were coming running from the neighbouring fields. Everybody was shouting, giving instructions to everyone else. Vas held his shoulder, wincing in pain, looking for the woman. Couldn't find her. People were already climbing up.

That's when he suddenly saw the old man. He saw that he was crying and a couple of other people were carrying the young woman. She was bleeding from the head. The old man, unhurt, was following her, limping. One side of her face was bloodied and she lay unconscious as people carried her and put her into one of the cars, obviously to be carried to the nearest hospital.

Vas stood transfixed, in a state of shock. The very shoulder that he was touching, it seemed to him that her neck was broken, as her face was tilted in a weird, horrible position.

All sounds receded. Everything around seemed somehow far. Vas stood numbed as the woman was being carried before his eyes, put onto a lorry and whisked away from his life, forever....

Then sound and motion returned and Vas's mind started to work at great speed. He limped back into the bus and managed to pull out his bag stuck under mutilated rexine seats. One of his shoes was missing, so he crawled back through the window to search for it. And in one stroke, when he put his head back into that bus, he actually, desperately, looked for the book by Ananthamurthy. Some people started screaming,

'GET BACK! Move away from the bus! It can go up in FLAMES!'

Her book! Where's her book? In a final desperate attempt, Vas wildly scavenged the rubble of the wrecked vehicle, the voices outside soaring; and just as he was about to give up, exit through the nearest window, he suddenly saw the book tossed amidst the waste, the small paperback, intact. In the maelstrom of the moment, Vas quickly left the ill-fated bus, scrambled out of the window through shattered glass, taking the book with him.

Vas was never to know the name of the young woman. He was never find out who she was. There were several people injured in that accident and also a few deaths.

The '*Later*' that she had promised, was never to happen later....

With a trashed shoulder, Srinivas Bhashyam rode off in a lorry towards the city of Bangalore, and started to read the first page of the *Short Stories of U.R. Ananthamurthy*.

 Birds

Twenty-ninth October
nineteen eighty-nine

The *kadiyaas* have been working in the house a whole month and nineteen days now. I can't take it anymore. This ruthless invasion of my privacy in my very own home; I want them out! All of them! To hell with it if the paint in the study isn't done yet! They've done the bedroom, the living room, bathrooms, the passage. *Bas*! That's enough!

'Memsaab, can I have seven hundred and fifty rupees more today for some fresh material?' says the contractor standing in the passage.

'Anything!' my eyes narrow. 'Anything! To get you out of here! You don't even have to complete the job; just take the money and disappear! Don't let me see your face again.'

I thrust the money onto his palm and bolt the door on his grinning face.

Creep! He has the nerve to smile when I'm so…so flustered! And heave a big sigh of relief.

When will I have my little loft back to myself? God! It's psyching me out, you know! Why the hell did I get into this plastic emulsion nonsense with concealed wiring…all this rubbish? I was more than happy with my seasonal whitewash. First day, scraping, second day, two coats of *choona* and third day, shift the furniture back in place. Sounded groovy! But this time I've put my foot into my mouth, so suffer! *Jhelo* it!

Third November

They're still here, the painters of course. But I now have a feeling they are winding up.

'Three more days, Memsaab, *phir hum soorat bhi nahin dikhayenge.* Come and check the wall besides the window and the roof which has to be filled in and cemented.'

'I've explained this to you ten times, Rameshwar. What more do you want me to check? I've got my bags packed. I'm leaving for the airport right now. I have a flight to Delhi leaving at 5.30. Please hurry up with all this!'

'Memsaab, just this wire here! I'm taking it straight across here for the telephone connections and giving you an extra socket for a table lamp or cassette recorder. Do you need a bulb there in that corner? I've already given you one above the left wardrobe, and can I remove this poster?'

'Please...Rameshwar, do whatever I've already explained to you. Do it all just as it is. Only remember — remember! Before closing the hole in the roof and cementing it, make sure that the birds are out. You know the birds have been building their nest right above here...no, you won't see it like this, you need to use a jhaaroo and make sure nothing is left up there before you plaster the open side.'

'Don't you worry about that. *Woh sab hum dekh ke karenge...aise-ich thhora na band kar dega dekhe bina.*'

'Okay, okay...now I just have to leave. I'll be back in three days and please, complete everything — everything — by then. Please! I'll settle the remaining amount when I return.'

46

I bolt through the door with my handbag, press the lift button in exasperation and buzz off in the cab waiting downstairs.

Sixth November
Evening

Boy! What a terrible flight that was. Thank god, I'm back home. Hopefully the paint job would be over by now. I turn in the key carefully and open the door slowly; switch on one light, and then the next. Open the door to the terrace and look at my plants; they're doing fine. Unlock my bedroom. Little Babushka, my baby is smiling her wicked smile from the wall. Devil! Touch wood!

Pull out my heels and slip into my flat rubber slippers, sink into the chaise lounge, rest my head back…oh, let me have a look at my study; they should have finished it by now. Y − e − a − h…now this is more like it! Neat and white and dry! Smelling of fresh paint. The wooden window frame doesn't have any ugly oil paint stains on it. They've done a good job. Poor guys, how I bullied them, made their lives miserable. Finally, it's me, and my house and the quiet once again. I step onto the terrace kitchen, switch on the light, and put water onto boil. A fresh paper filter gives me steaming hot coffee out on my balcony and look out at the sea for a long time.

'Hello…Who's that? Deepa? Yes, I'm back. Got in a little while ago. Fine! Yeah, Delhi was okay. I loved the three days of winter. Except that I was overly dressed for it; needn't have got that ambitious. I mean, it didn't snow this time up in the mountains. The flight, yes…no, no! It was awful! You know how they take you up there and then…all those *jhatkaa–matkaas*! Really, I hate their sense of humour! You know how I am. I have this fear of dying in a plane crash…. If only I knew how to fly…like birds…. What? Doordarshan? Yeah, I did. Yeah, Doordarshan was o…ka…y! Noncommittal. Sure! It'll work out eventually, I know it. Alright, listen, you carry on with that news, I'll speak to you in the morning,

The sound of distant waves, a cool breeze, the lights of Sea Rock Hotel and then beyond the creek, the Worli skyline. It's nice to be in the quiet of your home once again. A good print of *Rain Man* and I sleep with 'satisfaction' on my mind.

Seventh November
Ten past six in the morning

O…oh…it's the doorbell, I think, must be! Must be the paper-*wallah*! What the hell! It's only six in the morning. I'll get up later. I'd asked him to leave the paper on the letterbox without ringing the bell. It's only six am. I'll sleep till nine this morning.

I turn my side and try to go back to my slumber when suddenly there's a flutter, and then a chaotic, squeaky pounding on my window. What's that? No, it's not this window. The sound, sure enough, is somewhere here, and it's desperate. Birds!…Yes! That's right…it's birds…but there are no birds outside my window, and I thought they were gone now…the birds, and the nest…but…one second! I charge out of my bed into the living room. Nothing there….

Oh God! It's coming from the study! I plunge open the door of the study and stand dumbfounded. Horrified! Against the glass window two birds are hitting themselves repeatedly, falling around and hitting back at the windowpane again and again. I don't believe it. The nest has gone, the ceiling is closed and cemented…the nest, the babies, the birds…should have all gone by now! The nest…is…gone…the….

Oh shit! The babies! The babies are up there!

Birds carrying straws fly across and hit themselves against the bolted glass window. I'm horrified. Good god! The babies…are the babies up there? Still? In the ceiling? Please god, no. Don't let them be…please! I…I'm…what do I do now? I should open the window. No, it's no good opening the window…the ceiling is sealed. Let me at least open the window, even if it doesn't make sense.

In one desperate attempt I open the window, consoling myself that I'm at least doing 'something'. The two birds, probably the ones whose fledglings, oh god, are up there, start desperately and angrily fluttering and screeching in the study. Wall to wall — one end to the other — squealing…shrieking…squalling…desperately darting the room from corner to corner…hitting at the ceiling; again and again and again!

The babies! Dear god! They're looking for their babies!

I, like a helpless criminal, stand accused at the door, a lump in my throat, rising. It's a horrible sight! A horrible feeling! Damn it! Do something! I nudge myself. Pull myself together; darting towards the wooden chest where I might find a hammer or something in the hardware drawer. I must break open the ceiling and let the babies out. Stool! I need a stool. But I must get the birds out of the window first and then shut them out. Then break open the ceiling. How can I do that? I need a *salli*. This tiny little hammer is no good for the ceiling. For Chrissake, why can't the *bai* ever come on time? I need help.

The birds are shrieking and hitting relentlessly; not stopping. How can I get them out first, to be able to bring in a stool to break open the ceiling? I run around the little study in circles to drive the birds out. They flutter across my eyelashes, flap their wings against my hair, my arms, and my chest, but leave, they won't! I drag in a stool somehow and manage to get onto it in spite of the hollering of the winged creatures. With all my strength I hit at the ceiling with the hammer. A dent is made, bits of plaster and cement falling from it all over my hair, face…but it is only a dent. Frustrated and angry at myself, I fling my arms around once more to get the flying creatures out of my study. How can I help them if they won't help me! I did it! I did it! Yes…that's it…! No…! Out!…Out!…And I bang shut the glass window. Tight. As tight as I possibly can.

They are gone. For now. Disappear. But then, back they are, with a vengeance.

Angrier. Fiercer. More pathetic! Jesus! What have I done? Why the hell did I have to close the ceiling? I get on top of the stool again and start hammering further at the dent. It's the doorbell. Thank god! The *bai* is here. At last! She can find me something sharp and tough now to use as a *salli*.

No, it's not the *bai*, it's one of the painter fellows. What a blessing. I can't believe it.

'It's just 7.20 in the morning...what are you doing here so early?' It's one of the *kadiyaas*. I can't wait to get him inside the door.

'Rameshwar has asked me to check if you were back. He wanted to do the final *hisaab*.'

I try to find something like words....

'What have you done? The ceiling...the birds...the nest...here, here....' I drag him to the study. 'The babies...the baby birds...get them out immediately, they are stuck up there...break the ceiling! Why didn't you check that before cementing it? How could you be so bloody careless! So inhuman? They must be choking, the poor things! I had told Rameshwar at least a *hundred times* to make sure....'

'Memsaab, we filled up the ceiling the morning after you left. We did it, and Rameshwar never said anything about the.... He hasn't shown up the last three days. He's been in bed with fever. He sent me to collect the money.'

'So, break the ceiling...hurry! See how the birds are howling outside the window...it's their babies up there!'

'Memsaab,' the painter fellow spoke calmly, a little surprised at my dishevelled state.

'This wall was cemented three days ago. The cement has dried. Even if you break it, the babies, as you say...would be dead long back now, for lack of air.'

He handed me the bill as calmly as he spoke the words, and as quietly and unruffled, left through the door.

I drop onto the sofa outside the study. Three days ago? Three days the poor birds have been screeching outside the glass panes, yelling for their babies. For the last three days they've been hammering at the window! They say that when a human being dies, the near and dear ones lament for four days, and after the *chautha* they get back to their lives and try to forget their loss. Today is the fourth day. The fluttering and shrieking continues. Tomorrow, it will be all silent.

I crouch on the floor with a sense of cold wet cement...wrapping around my flesh...forming, firming, hardening...hardening....

Cementing up my breasts, my neck, my cheeks...eyelids....

 Bombay Central

The train stalled a little short of Bombay Central, had taken unnecessarily long to pull out. Jatin stared out of the window, taking in the smells of the approaching city. It was a wet, grey August night and the anticipation of a new life in a new city hadn't allowed him to doze off even for a moment, or try and wade off passengers pushing against him. He thought of reaching out a bit to steady his handbag which peeped out of the cluster of tossed luggage lying on the rack above his berth, which he had been occupying only partially; the rest had been taken up by three other passengers travelling without reservation.

Had he been in his own ilaaqa in Bhawani Mandi where he had lived the sixteen years of his life, he would have, for sure, known how to keep the entire berth to himself.

But here, in a train to Bombay, arriving for the first time, the first time ever out by himself, he wasn't certain if he should assert his rights on the one-way ticket he held in his hand to the land of his dreams.

Jatin pulled the window down to keep the rain from wetting his left shirtsleeve.

This was his second night on the train. He had been travelling two whole days and now, when he was just a little short of the main Bombay Central station, there was this interminable delay.

The man sitting diagonally across in a white kurta-pyjama, holding a small briefcase in his lap had been staring at Jatin for quite sometime now.

There was a gentle smile on his face that made Jatin feel somewhat uncomfortable in his window seat. Right opposite him was an elderly couple, in the process of shifting out towards the door, gathering haphazardly, their belongings. As the space in front emptied out, the man promptly shifted and occupied the seat across from Jatin.

The rain took turns to pour, then stop, and then come down in torrents again. So this is what the Bombay monsoon was all about, thought Jatin. The rains here were a way of life for nearly three months of the year. For those three months all life would alter and adapt to the condition the city was in. But for now, it had eased off, allowing passengers to get out and stretch their limbs.

The last station wasn't far now but it seemed like something more crucial was happening elsewhere on the tracks, keeping them from making a smooth gliding into the main station. This was somewhere between Parel and Mahalaxmi, someone remarked.

Some men got off to take a beedi break, and stood facing the adjoining tracks, taking a leak on wet sleeper wood slats. Beyond the multiple railway tracks the city lights flickered gently through the drizzle, holding the promise of a new life, thought Jatin. He had always associated the flickering of lights with his village, the large house he had left behind, his mother standing at the door, strong and resolute, bidding him farewell, her eyes reflecting the diyas she held in a thaali as she smeared a red tilak on her son's forehead:

'May God protect you, beta!'

Jatin had been staring through the barred window, half out of anxiety and half to avoid the constant gaze of the man sitting facing him. Amidst the din of the compartment and the patter of rain, he failed to realise he was being spoken to. With a jerk of his neck he turned his eyes towards the seat across and found that the man in the white kurta-pyjama was addressing him.

'Sorry, are you speaking to me, sir?' Jatin hesitated.

'Yes, you...,' he smiled assuringly, 'are you coming to Bombay for the first time?'

'Yes...and for the first time out of Rajasthan,' Jatin promptly replied and then, as promptly, realised that he should not be giving out information about himself more than was necessary to strangers. That was the pact between his mother and him. This was Bombay city, the big bad world of films. He was here to struggle, to make a life for himself as an actor. He would be meeting all sorts of people. He must watch out.

The man pulled out a pack of cigarettes from his pocket, unfolded the silver foil and put one to his mouth. From his other pocket he drew a matchbox. Then, as if on a second thought, he held out the pack to Jatin. Jatin looked at the red and white Charminar pattern on his palm, hesitated for a bit, then looking at the man's face, he decided to decline the offer.

'No, thank you. I don't smoke.' He said this with all of his sixteen years of Sainik School discipline, remembering the failed attempts at smoking that had ended up in long bouts of coughing in the boys toilet.

'Be firm when you say *no*! Your *no* should not sound like a *yes*' his mother again.

The man surveyed Jatin's face for a while, gauging his *no* with a slight narrowing of his eyes, then smiling, he drew back his hand. 'Good,' and went on to light his cigarette. Jatin gazed at the lights outside. 'Good,' the man mumbled more, making Jatin shoot a quick glance at him once again. The man took a deep puff at the cigarette and turned his head to look out of the window, the glass reflecting his clear image. Jatin saw that the man was in his mid or early forties, the rakish skin tone bearing evidence of a hard life. But something about him seemed endearing. The leather briefcase, the only luggage he carried seemed to suggest that he hadn't been out on a long journey and his unruffled appearance, despite the delay and the chaos of the compartment in the monsoon night, marked him as a frequent traveller on this route.

'Are you travelling alone?' asked the man without looking at Jatin.

The question, the answer to which was obvious, only implied that the man wanted to make small talk while waiting for the train to start moving again. There was something effeminate about him, noticed Jatin, as he settled into a comfort zone with the stranger.

'Yes.'

'What brings you to Bombay?'

'To...to work in films.... I want to be an actor.'

Just then the train jolt-started and slowly began to move, sending the lolling passengers hurtling back to their seats. Those out on the tracks leapt across and clung on to the metal bars on either sides of the doors. The 'Parel' signboard slowly glided past Jatin on his right. He sat back in his seat infused with fresh energy, his khaki handbag, swinging overhead, threatening to fall. He lunged again to push it back.

'Relax, it won't be long now,' said the man gathering his own briefcase as people squeezed back into their seats.

'You know, I myself wanted a life in films.'

'Really?' Jatin brightened up.

The man now leaned forward to speak to the young boy, who suddenly seemed to have found a new interest in him.

'Yes, I even joined a production company back in the eighties.'

Jatin's body language altered. He suddenly seemed more intent on the conversation. He wanted to know so much more about the world of cinema, about the life of the film people. He listened with rapt attention as the man went on to recall his brief stint with the movies. It was during his early days in the city when he'd worked as a production assistant in Kamalistan Studio during the filming of the epic *Razia Sultan*.

The train had picked up speed now and the lights of the city flashed past rapidly through the rain-drenched window.

'Do you know anyone in Bombay?'

'No.'

'Do you have a place to stay?'

'No, not yet....'

'Where will you stay the night?' There was almost a wistful note in the stranger's voice.

'I have...the name of a guesthouse in Dadar which is not very expensive. I'm supposed to stay there for the first two nights, and then I'll go to Andheri where I am to meet someone from my hometown who has promised to find me accommodation.'

A brief silence fell between the two. The man took a long drag at his cigarette, then, carefully suggested, 'You could come home with me....'

Jatin looked up, surprised. 'Oh no, that won't be necessary at all! I'm sure I'll find a taxi to take me to Dadar.'

'*Is barsaat mein*?' said the man, sizing up the lad. 'You are young, my dear boy, first time in the city...it is not safe out there. It is already so late; where will you go looking for a guesthouse in this rainy night?'

Jatin did not answer.

'Come, stay in my house for the night. I live very close to Bombay Central station. *Chalo*! It's almost walking distance...you can be my guest for tonight, tomorrow morning you can leave early and look for a place, or this relative that you know.'

For once Jatin got thinking. It *was* late...the man was right.

He looked at the man's face. There was something gentle about his manner; his concern was almost familial. He somehow felt reassured in the stranger's company. Yet, he hesitated before he spoke — his *no*, this time, being more of a *yes*.

'I really don't wish to cause any trouble to your family...I would hate to disturb....'

'My wife and I...it's just the two of us at home. We have no children. She will be more than happy to receive a guest as yourself.'

Jatin quickly calculated the options available to him at two in the morning. He had already made up his mind when he spoke next.

'But I would hate to be a burden....'

'It would be no burden at all! Let me be your host just for tonight...tomorrow morning, you can find your way to your new life.'

The train trundled into Bombay Central amidst the low grunted calls of coolies, passengers looking for relatives and the shuffling of luggage and handcarts. The man quickly gathered whatever little he had and then picked up the suitcase, khaki fabric covered that Jatin had pulled down from the overhead rack, and moved briskly towards the door, a little too eager-footed for the young boy still trying to find his bearings.

So he was finally here, in Bombay, the city of his dreams. Jatin looked around. Bombay Central station was huge. At the centre of the platform was an enormous clock, showing thirteen minutes past two in the morning. Even at this late hour, the pace of the city was decidedly different than anywhere else he'd been. For a while he stood, mesmerised by the enormity of his surroundings, the surge of passengers, the garbled announcements over the PA system.

Seeing the man carry his suitcase, Jatin leapt and grabbed it, then followed him down the broad staircase leading towards the exit. The man spoke animatedly about the city he lived in, and his work trips to Kalyan, as they manoeuvered their way through the throng of people rushing to make it through the exit, all at once. But this, probably being the last late-night train to arrive, the teeming platform drained itself of people as quickly as it had filled in.

Outside, the queue of taxis was down to a scanty few — barely two or three — and those too seemed to be quickly setting off with passengers, making Jatin somehow grateful for his decision of having accepted the man's hospitality for the night. As the rain showed no signs of abating, there was no question of walking to the house; Jatin's fabric covered suitcase being the other reason.

'Taxi-wallahs usually don't like to ply this short a distance; that's the trouble I face each time I land up at the station,' said the man, and then turned around to speak to a reluctant cabbie in Marathi.

Jatin could not understand what the men said to each other but he was relieved to see his new friend waving to him with the taxi door open, signalling for him to get inside. Once the taxi started, Jatin could not keep his eyes off the road — the buildings around Bombay Central were stunning examples of the old British architecture, the only other colonial structures he'd seen were the churches in Panchmarhi during his summer trips there.

Dazzling in the monsoon night, the overpowering monuments were nothing like he'd ever dreamt of. The roads were empty; just the sparkling stone structures gleaming in the rain made Jatin suddenly feel intimidated by his new surroundings.

The taxi moved through the shimmering streets, then a couple of turns into the small lane, it drew into a dark alley stopping at a cul de sac that unexpectedly appeared after making a quick left. In front was a rather humble structure of brick and cement, an old cottage, Portuguese style, somewhat run down, surrounded by tall buildings on all sides.

Getting out at once, the man paid the taxi driver an amount pre-fixed, then walked around to the other side and opened the door for the boy to step out. There was something obsequious in his manner that made Jatin a bit sheepish at already being treated like a celebrity. His struggle, though, would begin the next morning.

The man hurriedly lifted the wrought iron latch, unclipped the wooden gate and moved under the awning. With one hand on the flaky wall, he rang the doorbell. Jatin shook his head in an attempt to brush the rainwater off his hair. The man turned to look at him and smiled one more time, kind of appreciating Jatin for having accepted his invitation. He turned to ring the doorbell again. There was no answer.

'She may be asleep, sir...your wife,' said the gawky teenager, more as an attempt to fill up the awkward silence between the ring, and the long wait for the door to open.

'No, she never sleeps...when she knows I am returning.'

The man had a reassuring look on his face; the grace of a man confident of his place in life. Just like his mother, thought Jatin, self-willed, strong, alone, standing up for her son in the face of opposition, primarily from his father. If it wasn't for her, he may have never made it this far and this close to his dream.

The door opened. In the dim streetlight, beside a pale curtain stood a woman wearing a sari, her hair tied into a loose knot at the nape of her neck. She looked not much younger than the man, her gentle features though, defying her age. Seeing a young lad standing behind her husband, she quickly fixed her ruffled look and moved back into the shadow, allowing the two men to step in. The man turned towards the boy, and placing his hand on his shoulder led him into the house.

'This is Jatin, he is our guest for tonight.'

The woman switched on a light to make the room brighter, then, gently tucking her hair behind her ears, she turned around to register the young man.

Jatin bent his head and said namaste. The woman returned the gesture warmly, and then glanced at her husband who was looking intently at her for a reaction. They smiled at each other, an endearing smile, thought Jatin, between a man and his wife.

The couple was rather servile in the way they treated a guest even though the house seemed bereft of any kind of luxury. Jatin looked around a neatly done-up simple room — a television placed on top of a trolley facing a three-seater, a small coffee table with a lacy plastic tablecloth, a clean steel ashtray placed at the centre.

The food was laid out on a table outside the kitchen where the man and the boy quietly sat down and ate, the woman carefully serving each helping, insisting on her husband having a fluffed chapati straight from the fire onto his plate. Over dinner, the man spoke little to his wife; just a brief recount of the assignment he'd been out on. There was also some talk concerning the condition of the tin roof, which leaked incessantly due to the heavy rains that had already set in earlier than expected.

The conversation then steered towards Jatin's family, his home in Rajasthan and his starry aspirations. The man related incidents from his life when he had first migrated to the city years ago and how the couple had started out their life together with very little. Now, according to them, well settled, the man continued to put the bread on the table while the woman kept the home, meticulous.

The woman spoke little; a yes here and a nod there, ensuring that her participation in the conversation wasn't absent. From her expressions, she seemed to go along with most of what her husband said, taking regular breaks to serve the men well, the paan and sweets at the end of their meal.

A large clock on the wall struck three cords. As the two men got up to wash their hands over the sink, the host suddenly seemed in a bit of a hurry to wind up for the night.

He went on to make a bed for his young guest to sleep on, pulling a cot from the verandah into the living room. From inside the storage drawer set under the three-seater, he took out a cotton mattress and un-rolled it on the charpoy, then placed a clean sheet over the mattress. Jatin helped him pull up the charpoy next to the window from where the little garden and verandah outside were visible. Once the bed was laid out, the mosquito net nicely tucked in, and after making sure the young lad was going to be comfortable for the night, the man went inside the room.

The wife could be heard in the kitchen doing the dishes. As she came back to the table one last round, Jatin fidgeted around trying to help her with the clearing up, but the woman went about the routine without reacting to his presence.

In a brief while the man came out wearing a vest over a dhoti. For the first time Jatin noticed that he was a small-built man, rather lean at the shoulders.

'If you need to use the toilet at night, it's right there, behind you...behind that curtain,' he said while slipping his feet into a pair of Kolhapuri chappals. 'Switch on the first light on the left, and you'll see it,' he added, handing a pink face towel to Jatin.

'Thanks,' Jatin nodded gratefully, then searched his mind for appropriate words. 'Please don't worry about me...I just hope I won't disturb you, as I will be leaving early ....'

The man now stood looking at Jatin without saying a word. For a while Jatin looked on, waiting for him to say something. The man gazed at the verandah, then turning towards Jatin again, smiled.

'You've had a long journey two nights on the train...you must be really tired, my boy. I hope you sleep well.'

Inside the bathroom behind the yellow curtain, Jatin changed into a pair of khaki track pants and a t-shirt that he'd managed to pull out of his overstuffed handbag without completely unzipping it.

Winding up her nightly chores, the woman followed her husband to the verandah where he now stood under the tin shed looking at the bare little garden with a rusted wrought iron bench occupying the centre.

Jatin watched the couple pull down the jute cot under the tin shed and roll out another set of bed linen. The cot was placed at the edge of the shed so the spray from the rain would slightly wet the corners. The man looked much older now than what he had seemed on the train, thought Jatin. The couple sat talking for a bit and then the woman got up switching off the lights in the house.

Zipping up his bag after and checking the stuff he had to leave with in the morning, Jatin walked to his charpoy, placed the bag near the left leg and lay down, finally, to rest.

But sleep evaded him. His head was full of possibilities of a life he was going to build for himself in the city of Bombay. He would have to start somewhere, anywhere! He would take up any kind of job at the studio that his friend worked in at Andheri, and then find his way. His father hadn't been at all keen on his venture but he had had his mother's support.

'Go, follow your dream! Do what your heart tells you!' she had told him during those awkward years of pubescence. 'Life is full of surprises, learn to accept the challenges!'

Jatin lay in the dark, taking in the musty smell of the monsoon night; the whirring of the dark brown fan above, made dizzy his flow of thoughts, memories, faces, sounds....

It hadn't been long before sleep had taken over when something like a ruffle slightly shook him. With his eyes still closed, Jatin tried to remember the feeling, which would wake him in the middle of the night, the sense of falling from a great height, — or being jolted out of sleep…some such thing. He tried to return to sleep, but it was not a sound in his mind. The ruffle was finger felt. He felt it close, very close, creeping up on him.

Jatin tried to figure if there was a cat in the house he hadn't noticed earlier, trying to crawl onto his bed. But that very instant he shot his eyes open, caught in a petrifying moment. The woman was sitting at Jatin's bedside, running her fingers through his hair. He at once tried to get up but the pressure of her palm indicated he wasn't meant to do that. Little beads of moisture erupted on his forehead as he gulped soundlessly, lying still, in shock and fear.

Before Jatin could fathom what was going on, the woman slid herself under the mosquito net, aligning her body next to his, causing the young boy to rapidly break out into a cold sweat.

Jatin tried to raise his body in an attempt to break away from her, but as soon as he lifted himself to sit up, the woman held him down by placing her arm across his chest.

Jatin lay still, his heart pounding crazily inside him, petrified to make even the slightest of moves. His forehead was drenched more from perspiration than from the spray hitting him through the jute-crossed window. But he dared not utter a sound. He allowed her hand to run along his smooth un-hairy chest, leading down towards the string of his khaki track pants. A sudden sensation took over, startling the boy into a terrifying awakening.

Outside, the rain came down in torrents. Jatin's eyes darted towards the verandah where the husband slept soundly under the tin shed, oblivious of the mayhem taking place in his young guest's life.

The man shifted in his cot. Jatin froze. He could only sense doom; his world coming to an abrupt end. 'Please...your husband...he...he...could wake up!' Jatin managed a whisper, his body trembling at the woman's touch.

'No, he won't...,' she hissed in a tone unfamiliar to Jatin, and then like a cat's stealthy long stride, she moved, her weight on her right knee and slid her body over his.

Like a lioness she mounted the young boy, her sari gathered around her full hips. Jatin's taut nerves quivered beneath the woman's flesh.

The rhythm of her body steadily notched up, causing the wooden edge of the cot to repeatedly hit against the steel trunk, the charpoy shifting a little with each thrust. Lying beneath her, Jatin felt his entire body twitching, her hair all over his sweaty face. She mumbled words in a language he could not understand. He felt as if she was swearing at herself; her hissing, loud, incoherent to his ears, driving him to the edge. He wanted to shut his eyes and concentrate only on the flood of new sensations erupting within his unrehearsed body, but he could not keep his gaze away from the woman's face; she was now like an untamed animal jumping over him, her face distorting, gasping in wild ecstasy.

The image that flashed across Jatin's eyes at that moment was one he'd seen in his village — of a woman 'possessed', being hauled by the villagers, screaming and swearing words, understood by none. That somehow did not, at this particular moment, baffle Jatin as it had in his childhood. In fact, it was only now that he recognised it, and understood it, — only in this one flash of a moment, and it mattered least what she mumbled as long as the rhythmic rattle of the cot was rising constantly to a deafening din...a frenzy of sound and sensation rising above all else...and...and finally, finally...a cloudburst!

The rain had ceased by the time Jatin gathered his senses and scrambled out of bed, groping in the dark towards the bathroom door behind the yellow curtain.

Had he fallen asleep? That was impossible. Was it day yet? Jatin shuffled into the clothes he'd been wearing earlier that evening, which he had left folded on the three-seater. Without switching on the light he went inside the bathroom, turned on the tap, and splashed water on his face. The mirror in a green plastic frame showed a broad, stately forehead, sharp nose and large captivating eyes set in deep brown skin. His hair fell loose around his neck giving him the appearance of neither boy nor man.

And now, so much had changed, in just one instant. So much of what he had imagined would happen in other ways, had happened in this unpredictable way. It wasn't meant to be like this! It was supposed to be more 'meaningful' as his mother had always explained. Was there meaning to this? Is this how it was meant to happen? Without meaning...in a stranger's house...with a stranger's wife?

Where was the woman?

Jatin felt somewhat relieved at not having to confront her. And the man. What about the man? Would he have seen them in the night? Had he slept through all that had happened? No! That would be impossible.

Jatin ran his fingers over the stubble that seemed to have appeared overnight around his smooth chin. His movements became hurried and nervous, thinking how his mother would react if she were to ever find out how her son had lost his virginity. Jatin felt anxious, as he wanted get away from this place before either of the two people in the house woke up. He'd have to leave because he couldn't face them: neither the man, nor the woman. It would be better he left without them knowing.

The sky outside the verandah was still dark. Little drops of rainwater trickled from the tin roof and splashed on the cement floor. Jatin hurriedly packed his chappals, gathered his towel, folded his track pants and squeezed them into the bag without bothering to fully unzip it. He looked around for a sign of the two people in the house but did not see either of them.

The night still fell around him like an unsolved mystery. Finally, he picked up his bag, adjusting the strap across his shoulder. Then without making a sound, he walked across the living room, towards the door.

A sudden movement in the verandah made him turn around. Jatin saw the man walk up to the edge of the shed and stand against the wooden column. Slowly he pulled out a cigarette from his pocket and lit it. Jatin stood still.

Just then the woman walked up from behind and put her arms around her husband. She stood clinging to him, her head resting on his back. Without turning, the man reached out and held his wife. Jatin just stood there, looking at the two of them, astounded.

Why hadn't the man dragged him out of that bed and thrashed him? Why hadn't he thrown him out of the house? Beaten him to pulp? Killed him?

Had he not been aware of what was going on? In his own house? With his wife? Or had he...oh, my god!...*known*...!

Jatin stood frozen to the ground, his mind unable to fathom this....

The night was deep and silent. Jatin groped his way back to the main door. He turned the latch and let it slide down, soundlessly. Then with a slight pressure on the left side, he pushed open the wooden doorway.

A shaft of light streamed in from the streetlamp. Stepping out, Jatin placed his handbag on the floor, then, to lock the door behind him, he turned around, and stood...it was the most beautiful sight he'd ever seen. In the white-light filled verandah, the man and his wife lay together, their bodies curled up in a foetal position.

Jatin stood bewildered, trying to assimilate all that flashed through his mind at that moment. With the awakening of someone who'd suddenly grown up and in one instance, understood the complexities of life. In a flash of a moment life revealed itself to him in all its greys; he began to understand the aberrations...things his mother would never be able to explain to him in all his growing years.

As Jatin stepped out on the wet pavement at Charni Road, he was ready, ready to make a new start. Out there was a world unknown to him, and he at sixteen, having suddenly come of age, was now a young man, prepared.

 The Morning After

The bus rode along the narrow winding road into the far stretched valley, through thick clusters of tall elegant pines, fading into the shadows of the setting sun. The deep orange and purple light illuminating from the sky outlined the edges of the hills. It was gradually turning into shades of grey. The trees were still, as if in meditation, but a light breeze played with them every now and then.

Lily rested her head against the window and gazed at the star-studded hills, the dark, mysterious pines now beginning to sway with the breeze. A cool gush of wind fluttered through her hair as she pushed the clutch and opened the window. Yes, it smelled so good, the very mountain air, and she could see clearly the tiny huts with slanting black slate roofs scattered far and near along the road, with kerosene lamps burning in their interiors.

Lily turned her head when the bus slowly moved around a corner and stopped close to a couple of wayside shops. A man sitting across had seen Lily look around in confusion.

'It's not Ghuggar yet, Memsaab,' he said.

'Oh thanks,' she settled back, and started to gaze out of the window again.

Ghuggar...yes, she had so often thought of Ghuggar, but had never gathered enough courage to make the trip up here. It had been four years now and she wondered if it had been worth the while to have waited this long; if she had been unwise these past years. And suddenly Lily felt uneasy.

The bus now drove around the curve of the hill entering another valley, into a most beautiful spectacle. This was Ghuggar, she knew, a deep valley surrounded by mountains on all sides, not very high, but they sort of guarded the little village most preciously. So this is where she lives, thought Lily, perhaps a little enviously, much to her chagrin. But soon she got rid of the thought as the bus stopped in front of a small shed. A few people could be seen ambling around.

A coolie rushed to her aid as she stepped off, gracefully draped in a printed beige sari.

'*Kithhu jaana,* Memsaab?' he asked lifting the suitcase. Lily looked around her closely and then at the coolie.

'Oh, it's...it's the house of a woman called...Dolma,' she said as her hands moved restlessly over her handbag; she knew she was nervous.

'Dolma!' A whisper ran through the air among the few people around who were watching this lady who looked to be a pretty tourist. The coolie seemed a bit hesitant at first but then started to walk ahead without a word and Lily followed behind. The road was now dark and it was getting chilly.

'It gets cold here at night, Memsaab,' he said with a little lilt in his accent. Lily felt as if the coolie had not exactly the intention to say that, but she smiled.

'Is it a long walk?' she asked.

'Na, Memsaab...na...na...,' he nodded his head.

After about ten minutes of walking they approached a tea stall on the side of the road going uphill. A couple of people broke their conversation mid-sentence to watch the lady in a sari, as the coolie bent at the hanging rope lighter to light his beedi.

'There's the house, Memsaab,' shouted the coolie as he walked up hurriedly puffing at his beedi and pointed to a cottage a little away from the roadside towards the left, surrounded by pine trees on all three sides. Towards the corner on the right were a couple of shabby looking huts. One could see the interiors of some of them, where women sat weaving and cooking. Lily walked past and stood in front of this little house. Not too bad for a schoolteacher, she thought. The door was closed and she could hear a loud voice inside, that of a woman.

'This is it, Memsaab,' and the coolie put the suitcase on the steps, lifted his topi and scratched his head while Lily rummaged for coins in her handbag for a tip.

'Are you here to see the old lady, Memsaab?' he asked, as she placed some change on his palm.

'No, the young....'

Suddenly something smashed inside and an angry old woman charged out of the house shouting abuses in Dogri.

'I'm here to see her daughter, Dolma!' Lily quickly answered the coolie, who stood perplexed. Lily couldn't decide how she should greet the woman. She hesitated.

'Dolma is dead!' shouted the old woman.

Lily stood shocked staring at her. Dead? How could that be? She had come all this way to see her...and Dolma...she...she....

No! She didn't believe it...why?...when?...how?...and what about...?

She began to feel dizzy and stumbled towards the railing for support. The old woman looked at her, detached. She was a typical pahari woman, dressed in a worn-out shawl around her frail body, a faded printed scarf over her head with beads hanging around her neck. Though her body language seemed sharp, her eyes were dim.

'Dolma is dead?' Lily stared at the woman, her eyes full of disbelief.

'Yes, she is dead! And it doesn't matter anyway! After all the shame she brought to our community. She was one of us, and she brought disgrace to us poor people…and that little brat she left behind…that…her…I don't know what to do with that little monster!'

Lily winced. *My God, how the people responded to the very name of Dolma.*

'With the kind of money she made from the school,' continued the old woman, 'she wouldn't have lasted herself and that rascal very long anyway…. God knows where he came from! God only knows! And God only will help him! I'm going to have nothing to do with him…oh, no…not me. No longer can I put up with this disgrace…this shame!' And then suddenly she stopped. She lowered her voice and walked closer to Lily.

'Come inside, *bibi*…and…who are you?'

Without answering, Lily picked up her suitcase and walked towards the inside of the house. The coolie who had been standing in silence, turned to leave, when she called out, 'Coolie, can you come in the morning…*paanch baje*…*pehli* bus?'

'Ji, Memsaab!' he nodded and then walked away into the dark road counting the change in his hand.

Lily stepped inside the house. It was a grotty little interior. The walls were a burnt, dark wood and to the corner on the right, was a small part of the floor used as kitchen, where the fire burnt. Clothes lay scattered all over the place, and towards the right opened a window. A charpoy stood against the wall on the left with a rough chequered blanket hanging on one of its legs.

'It's getting colder,' said the woman rubbing her hands around her shoulders, standing out in the verandah, as she pulled the kerosene lamp off the iron hook and carried it inside, closing the door behind her. Lily stood in the centre of this, sort of small room, carefully holding on to her suitcase. She noticed another door adjacent to the kitchen, which perhaps led to another room. Around her right shoulder she firmly clutched on to her handbag. Her straight black hair fell to her waist.

'How did she die?' Lily's voice was shaky and low.

'Fever...cold! Fever!' The old woman came and stood close to her.

'Khoobsurat ho, bibi!' and she held the lantern up to Lily's face. Then placed it at the windowsill and sat beside the fire, warming herself.

Yes, she was pretty, thought Lily. Pretty for a thirty-one-year old widow! Money could preserve a woman's looks they say, but Lily had hardly looked carefully into the mirror since her husband's death. And that was a little over four years now, but seemed like ages...living in that big house all by herself! All that time she had been thinking of coming up here to see Dolma, and now finally when she was here...oh god! She pressed her hand against her forehead and placed the suitcase beside the wall.

The old woman pulled the charpoy down. 'Will you have some food?' she asked, spreading a dirty blanket over it. The old woman waited for an answer. She then drew a sheet from the trunk and smoothened it over the blanket, which definitely gave it a more comfortable look.

Lily stood quiet. 'No, I ate something on the way.'

'Will you have some chai, then?' She placed a pot of water on the log stove, and waited for it to come to a boil. Lily sat down on the cot and watched the fire burn. She had at once wanted to ask so many questions that had crowded her mind ever since, but all she could do was quietly look up and ask, 'Amma, where is...the boy?'

The old woman narrowed her brow and looked at Lily questioningly.

'I am a friend...of Dolma's,' she said most unconvincingly, while her fingers meddled with the metal clip of her bag.

'What have you come here for? Dolma didn't have a friend in the world! Everyone despised her. That's what the city did to her. Some big city, they say. Not that I know of, but she sure had a hard time, keeping alive that bastard!'

'Please....' Lily at once stood up. Her face was trembling, so were her hands. She looked at the old woman with almost beseeching eyes.

'Don't...please, call him that. I knew his father,' she managed in a voice barely more than a whisper.

The shaft behind the kitchen floor slowly opened and a little boy's face appeared in the doorway, with eyes wide and innocent. For a moment Lily stood dumbfounded looking at this beautiful picture in dirty clothes, but yes, there was mischief in his eyes, and she was at once startled by the resemblance! The eyes, the nose, the cheekbones...everything...everything the same...oh god! Her heart cried out.

The boy gaped at her.

'Handsome little fellow,' she thought gazing at him.

'Come,' she said and smiled at that face. One moment his eyes sparkled with curiosity and the very next, they reflected defiance as he saw the old woman staring at him.

'Get back inside, you...you...there's going to be no food for you tonight...not until you learn to behave yourself! I've had enough of you. Now get inside there!'

She nearly jumped at him and the boy ran back into the room slamming the door behind him, almost on the old woman's face.

'*Khotta*!' she shouted in anger, calling him names again, and then sat down again to make tea. Tiny sparks flew around as the woman blew into the half-burnt wooden logs. Her face, flushed with anger, appeared even redder in the glow of the fire.

'Strong features,' thought Lily. 'So, she is *her* mother.' She stood by the edge of the charpoy, wrapped up in her thoughts. The woman poured the tea in the two glasses placed on the floor, then added with her hands little pieces of jaggery.

'*Bibi*, you knew his father, you said, and how did you know him?' she asked handing out the glass of tea to Lily.

'He was my...husband.'

The glass in the old woman's hand shook, spilling the tea all over the floor. She quickly placed it down and wiped her scalded hand with the end of her shawl. She stared at Lily, her eyes wide with astonishment!

Lily walked over to the window and looked out.

'I shall not stay long...I had come to see Dolma...to make some arrangements for her child...I will leave early in the morning,' she stated, still looking out at the night sky now quickly filling up with grey clouds.

'Amma, I have come to give Dolma's son his due...I want to fix up a part of my husband's money for the boy. For his education...food...clothes...his future,' her voice choked.

'Since he is my husband's only child...'

Tears flushed her eyes as she finished her sentence. 'I have no child of my own.'

Lightning flashed across the sky and a few minutes later it was raining heavily down the windowpane.

'The weather here, you never know when it changes,' said the old woman and lay a bed for herself on the floor, where she coiled in, sipping hot tea. Every now and then she glanced at Lily who still stood by the window.

'You want to support your husband's *bastard* child? I do not understand; you are strange,' she watched Lily with a considerable amount of apprehension.

'What about the boy?' Lily turned towards the door and asked. 'He hasn't eaten, has he?'

'No,' answered the old woman. 'It's getting very late, go to bed now,' she muttered, sliding inside her blanket.

It was now barely drizzling and Lily was wide awake at two in the morning. Her chai lay on the windowsill, ice-cold. She sat at the edge of her bed, puffing at her cigarette. She had picked up smoking only after Ravi's death. Funny, she never thought she'd need it though. And Ravi, yes, she thought of Ravi. Ravi, whom she had married going by her parents' wishes, after a prolonged childhood of twenty-one years. 'You will never grow up,' her mother always said, and now, now it was different. In fact, it had been different after marriage. Ravi had been such a playboy, while she had been happily unaware. And then he had told her of Dolma's condition, and Lily's world had shattered.

Though Ravi had often tried to convince her that he didn't love the girl, but had simply taken a fancy to her, and that it had all been a betrayal of the moment, Lily could never understand this kind of reasoning and compromise. The thought, even after knowing that Dolma had gone away with her baby to her home in the hills, had constantly tortured her. More so when she was left all alone in this world, shortly after Ravi died in a car crash. She had felt sorry for him at times, and at times extremely angry, to the extent of being neurotic, but she still cared for him like a faithful wife.

Clouds thundered once again in the sky, and Lily sat back on her bed with her legs cuddled up. Just then the door near the kitchen opened, and the little boy walked in and stood beside Lily, while she made a futile attempt to get rid of her cigarette.

'You still awake?' she asked an obvious question.

For a moment he just looked, and then said, 'Are you afraid of the lightning?'

'No, are you?'

'No....' he answered and shook his head a couple of times. She knew he was afraid.

'Are you hungry?' she asked, stubbing out the cigarette against the wooden leg of her charpoy.

'Oh, no, no,' he said and looked away. Just like Ravi, she thought again. Defiant and self-willed. Her lips broke into a faint smile.

'Won't you sit down?'

'No.'

'Why...?' Lily was curious.

'I don't know you.'

'Oh.' Lily backed off.

Then, an awkward silence.

'Did you know...my mother?'

'*Huun*...yes.'

'Did you...like her?'

Lily was surprised at the question and suddenly felt sorry for the little boy. God! He'd never known anyone to even remotely like his mother. Maybe all he has ever known is despise and hatred and abuse! Lily reached her hand out to him. His eyes were anxious and wide in anticipation of an answer, and yes, all this rebuke had taken away a bit of his innocence, she thought, as she looked closer. But he did not respond to this brief gesture of friendship, and Lily, after a tiny moment of thought, withdrew.

'You haven't told me your name yet,' she tried to sound casual.

'Manu. That's what my mother called me,' he said almost forgetting that Lily hadn't answered his previous question.

'Manu! That's a cute name,' she smiled, gaining ground.

'Do you want to see my mother? I have her in a picture.... '

After a little hesitation, Lily followed Manu in through the little door behind the kitchen. This was Dolma's room; she knew the moment she stepped in. It was neater than the rest of the house and well kept. There were drapes on the window, hinting at her brush with city life.

'That's Ma!' Manu pointed to a photograph in a small frame on a corner table beside the divan. Lily walked up to it and saw. God! She was beautiful!

Lily sensed, inside her, a feeling she had not known before. She wasn't jealous, as she had imagined she would be, when she'd meet Dolma, but instead, she felt a sense of awe for the woman in the picture.

A fair skinned, pahari looking, very pretty young woman with dark hair and features, not so sharp, but a peculiar warmth exuding from her eyes. This was Dolma.

Lily couldn't understand her own feelings at that moment. This woman, she had ever so despised, was so different from Lily's idea of the 'other woman' she'd carried in her mind. She was unmistakably touched by her fragile looks and gentle warmth. She turned to look at Manu who stood gazing at his mother's photo. Yes, she thought, Manu's mother had been brave; brave for a girl to have borne a child out of wedlock, all by herself. Maybe unhappy, but she surely must have been proud of her little boy. And Manu did look so much like Ravi, she thought again. Those same large eyes, wheatish skin, and sharp nose.

'Yes, I liked your Ma....' Lily spoke almost to herself and Manu's little face broke into an enchanting smile. 'Oh, Ravi...Ravi...,' her heart murmured.

'Will you have something to eat, Manu? I know you are hungry,' and without waiting for an answer this time, Lily walked back into the kitchen. The fire was dying but she managed to cook some dal and rice for him. When she walked back into the room, Manu had opened the back door, which led to a little verandah outside, covered with a small tin roof. The view from there was mystifying. You could see the edge of the hill and the lights of the village beyond. It was drizzling still and the night was cold.

'I like the rain.' Lily spoke while Manu had started to eat. 'Do you?'

'Yes...I do...will you stay with us?' Manu asked with his head bent over his plate.

'No, I have to leave in the morning,' she watched him eat.

'Leave, for where?' he looked up at her.

'For Delhi,' she answered, and nearly hoped she didn't have to leave that soon.

Manu stopped eating. 'Ma was in the city...Delhi, she said...is it nice there? Nani always says, the city is a rotten place, has bad people.'

Lily clutched her hands together as she suddenly felt a chill, standing out in the open.

'You will find good people and bad people everywhere, Manu,' and she once again fell back in her long stream of thoughts.

Someone was knocking on the front door. The old woman woke up. It was 3.40 in the morning. Who could it be? She quickly picked up the lantern and held it up as she opened the door. There was the coolie, standing there with a thick gunny bag on his head.

'*Biji*, tell the Memsaab, it's time to go.' He spoke shivering.

Lily had heard his voice and come into the room. Her eyes were tired from sleeplessness.

'I'm coming, Coolie, what time does the bus leave?'

'At 4.20, Memsaab,' and he rubbed his hands in quick motion.

'Amma, I will send the money for Manu, and for you, every month,' and she walked back into the other room where little Manu lay fast asleep on the couch. She stopped in the doorway. No, she wouldn't wake him up she thought, and then glanced at Dolma's photograph. Her warm face looked back at Lily, and Lily could see in a small frame what life was all about. The thoughts that had tortured her for four long years suddenly seemed so worthless, so unkind, because all she ever thought of was her own suffering, her own failure. That disappointment, in her mind, had buried the burning truth of this short span of life, and Lily had let herself be tightly gripped by the darker side of things. But, in fact she had always been in search. In search of the brighter side, and now she had found it. In the small picture frame. Yes, this little frame that spoke of acceptance of the darkness, of the urge to continue to survive.

And Lily was a different person.

'Are you leaving?' Manu was sitting up in his bed looking at her. Lily walked up to him and knelt down beside him. Manu put his hand on her shoulder gently and repeated, 'Are you going away?' His face reflected disappointment. Lily was silent for another moment and then she spoke.

'Yes, Manu, I have to leave now.'

Manu drew his hand back. Lily touched his little chin. 'Will you come with me?' she asked. Manu looked at her face.

'With you? To the city?' His eyes began to shine in the semi darkness.

'Yes, if you'd like to stay with me....'

'Oh, can I?...can I?...' and Manu flung from the couch.

Lily quickly dressed him in warmer clothes and soon, they were out in the room where the old woman was waiting for her.

'Manu is going with me, Amma!' Her expression gave away her feelings. Manu come and stood beside Lily. The old woman stared at the two speechless. By now the coolie had carried the suitcase to the gate and was waiting for Lily. Lily turned back to say goodbye to the old woman.

'You sure are strange, *bibi*.' She spoke in a low voice as Lily stepped down holding her bag in one hand, Manu's hand in the other. And then Manu tugged at her hand.

'Wait, I have to get something from inside,' and he ran back into the house. When he returned he was holding two objects in his hands which he held up to Lily's face: one was her packet of cigarettes and the other was his mother's face in the photo frame.

'You will need this,' he said, handing the packet to her.

'No, wait,' said Lily. She flung the packet of cigarettes across the hillside. 'We won't need that anymore,' she smiled. 'Come!'

'No, wait...I don't know you...who are you?'

'A friend,' and Lily bent to kiss his tiny forehead. 'Call me Lily Aunty!' and the two walked out on the road.

The fog around the dark trees was splitting a new day was about to break....

❦

 The Mad Tibetan

The January snow starts to flake off the mountain peaks. *Karas* has formed over the freezing waters of the river. A stinging wind wafts across the valley of Ladakh. The little Ladakhi boy who comes to my room to replenish the bukhari, the handmade heater with fresh logs of wood, looks out of the window pointing to the lights across the river, but says nothing. He just stares at the snow peaks and then turns towards me. I move out of my bed and stand next to him, seeing what he sees. In a valley, still blue with the night, tiny lights glimmer on the mountainside. I stand mesmerised by the sight beyond the mercurial shimmer of the river.

'What's that?' I ask with a small movement of my hand.

The eight-year-old stands gaping at me with tiny, speaking eyes, and then moves back to the bukhari.

'Stok,' he says softly, stoking the fire.

I sit at the edge of my bed watching his face in the orange glow. His cheeks are a burnt red; they flush with the light as he tilts his little head and puffs into the flame. After he is done, he leaves the room without looking up even once. He has learnt to communicate with strangers who trek the vast desert landscape during the winters, looking for, themselves.

I walk back to the window again.

'Stok…' I muse.

I haven't slept all of last night. It was that sound again, of something uneasy; the constant drone of it, piercing through the night; at times right up close, just over my shoulder; at times, moving far away. I've been woken up by this eerie sound, like something rattling in my head, and not been able to go back to sleep again. I wonder if I've been imagining it…I cannot tell, but the last few nights have been unsettling.

I am in this little place called Agling, a tiny settlement of precisely three houses set amidst winter-yellowed fields. I've been here in a room by the river for the last nine days, walking around with my camera, exploring the terrain, seeing what the winter does to the landscape, the colours it takes away, the shades it brings in. I'm here because I so needed to get away.

From my first floor window I sit and gaze out at the slopes across. I see the hazy spread of tenements clinging to the edge of the snowline. Stok. I was struck by it when I first drove to it two years ago and I'm still fiercely drawn to it, its brazen beauty imprisoned in my mind. But most of all, I like to sit by the rocks and listen to the rippling of the river, its soft rush of the water. This is the Indus, which finds its way down from Mt. Kailash, in the vicinity of Lake Mansarovar, flows placidly through the valley of Ladakh and then enters Pakistan via the northern regions of Gilgit and Baltistan. I can walk down and touch it…its frozen banks glistening in the blue night.

Morning comes in crisp and fresh. The sky starts to clear. The day seems promising; the light is just right. Taking stock of my itinerary, I wrap myself in a yak's wool muffler, my Canon EOS 50 slung across my shoulder, the cotswool gloves and most important, the double-rotis — two thick wheat-pancakes stuffed with dry kidney beans — folded and slid inside the inner pocket of my parka, and I'm all set…I'm not sure exactly for what; a photographer is never really sure.

I start with the exterior of the house…a pot of water left to boil out in the backyard now covered with snow, a bicycle, tilted; a black dzo, its reflection upside down in the sparkling waterway; two Ladakhi women, camera shy, walking along a grey stone wall….

I cross the bridge and start to ascend the vast pebbled slope stretching across the river towards the village of Stok. Here, more images: burnt, twisted tree-trunks along the stream, frozen in its fall; empty rusted tin cans that hang from bare wet branches; the little temple of Kali, her large eyes glistening in the soft light; the face of an old woman in a window; a tattoo on the wall of the Stok Palace.

It is half past three in the afternoon by the time I cross the bridge at Choglamsar and start walking back towards Agling along the old army road. The sky is different now. The glister of the morning, the moist white sun is giving way to a blue that is beginning to engulf the vast mountainous terrain.

Sitting here, just a few steps down on the rocks by the river, I watch the evening set in. I sit looking, listening, waiting…for something to happen. The light changes several times. A restrained yellow glow at first, then a deep redness, and then the dark…a darkness, a redness quite enchanting, and yet…something else, perhaps? I don't know what, but I wait. Knuckled around me in a circle is the snow all over the mountains, the brown barrenness of slim branches between the river and the slopes, and a sudden black of a yak here and there, for the dramatic element.

A low chopper has been circling overhead with a deafening whirring sound. Once it moves away, the river will come back to me. The prayer flags weather beaten, hanging from the little bridge, change colour. A woman on the other side of the river walks over pebbles with five yaks behind her, all in a hazy black. Two ropes dangling from the bridge, immersed in water, the edges dripping, drifting with the breeze…and then it happens. The colour, it changes once again.

This time, from near darkness to a silvery glow, which begins to emerge from behind the mountains. And before I can sharpen my senses to this transition, I find myself in 'moonland'! Awestruck, I watch the dusty black mountainscape turn to clear metallic, the colour of smooth steel; a steelness that dips the entire valley in its hue, sinks to my innermost being and settles in there.

I feel more and more like a nomad!

Far out on my left, by the glassy-white riverbed, I see something; a tent, is it?...yes, a tent. And besides that, some children playing, sprinting about laughing; appearing, disappearing into the mist, their laughter rippling across the white landscape.

'Tibeti!' says a voice. I look up. The woman with the five yaks re-emerges from the mist. I get up, cross the barbed wires and begin to walk towards the tent.

Little red-cheeked Ladakhi boys come running and playfully start throwing stones at the man inside, giggling and squeaking. Their shrill, high-pitched voices fill the empty expanse with strange phonetic sounds:

'Nyonba!...Nyonba!'

A man in a deep red overcoat comes rushing out of the roofless tent. He lurches at the boys swearing, flinging his arms in the air; chasing them back towards the barbed wires. Not so easy to be dissuaded, the little brats stumble, hurdling over each other, shrieking, picking pebbles from the ground, throwing them at him in turns.

'Nyonba!...Nyonba!'

I change the lens on my camera and carefully skirting around the scene, move in closer to where the action is. The Tibetan's scrawny face looks startled at the sight of a woman. I lower the lens. He stands before me, glaring. I step back. Oh, oh...I shouldn't be encroaching...but then, he smiles, a clear disarming smile, like the tinny waters of the river. I...smile back, raise the camera again, look through the lens and click. A smile gets frozen in a rectangle.

I turn around to focus on the kids when I hear a voice. The man is saying something, in Tibetan, I assume. He points towards me, towards...my camera? Yes, he is pointing at my camera. What? I lift the camera up to him. You want this? He nods anxiously. Can't hand it to him, can I?...or perhaps, why not...I start to pull the strap off my neck, walking back towards him. But no, he doesn't want the camera; he is seeking my attention. He stands with one hand on the hip, the other on his tall fur hat, then turns towards me and smiles! Again, he repeats the gesture; hand on the hip, fixes his hat, turns, smiles! Oh, he is posing for me! He wants me to take his picture...oh, how sweet! Yes, of course!

I move in closer, with not so much trepidation this time and hold the lens to his face. The sound of the click somehow thrills him. He wants something else. He scuttles around to the back of the tent, indicating for me to follow him. Against the light he now stands, pointing to the frozen river in the back. Ah! The river for backdrop...perfect! I look through the lens and click again. In my 24mm wide, the Tibetan stands in his deep red overcoat with loose sleeves, black beads around his neck and a flapped fur hat protruding on either sides of his ears. Through the burly black locks, I grab his dark face — the features, perfect, his eyes, slanting, misleading a bit....

Something about the Tibetan fascinates me. The lean, agile figure now starts to do things, strange and startling.

I switch to telephoto and move in further, focusing on him, clicking; capturing his each movement, each expression. He winces, gleams at my intrusion, then ducks down into the tent. I skirt around him trying to peek inside, but see nothing. Suddenly he springs up, grinning! I shriek! Sheepishly, I step back, embarrassed at not being savvy enough to keep up with his delightful shenanigans. A little game starts to play between the Tibetan and me. He is performing, peacock-like, strutting about, showing off all his colours; the flashing of his dark narrow eyes...his bewitching smile! Each monkeyshine of his, I'm supposed to be alert to and capture with my lens; freeze the moment with quick flashes! Smile! Click! Duck! Click! Frown! Click! Eye-shine! Click! Hide! Click! Oops! Both giggling!

This man is a performer! An actor! Perfect subject for a photographer!

His face is a burnt bark-brown, squalid, wrinkled, the skin of old yaks. His eyes have the look of one who has lived many lives. Is he young, is he old, I cannot tell....

Suddenly it begins to snow. Damn! Hurriedly I tuck the camera under my muffler. Little gossamers of white slowly start to fill the landscape, turning it to a bluish grey.

The Tibetan is looking up at the sky, the smile from his eyes gone; the expression on his face now decidedly undecipherable. Suddenly he runs inside the tent, darts down to the bare ground, and fiercely begins rummaging through his things. I follow; try to peep in. Hair all over his face, he is on all fours, scrambling the floor for something. The low, grunting sound immediately puts me at unease. What could he so frantically be grabbling for?

Between the grunting and grinding of his teeth, when I catch his face he appears like a wild animal, hunting...or hunted...something like that.

Suddenly he springs to his feet, breathless, holding in his hand, a matchbox! His eyes are wild. He grins! A matchbox? I'm perplexed. I sort of, grin back. Inside me, I am slowly beginning to freeze...from the chill. My hands start to shiver. I need to rub my palms together, get the flow back.

A strong wind starts up; the soft snow quickly turns to sleet.

He is oblivious of my presence now: all crouched up in front of the mud stove, striking matchsticks, trying to light a fire in the falling snow. I'm befuddled. The matchsticks won't light. He strikes again, and again, and again, ferocious as a tiger, growling fiercely, the white snowflakes falling around him, filling the roofless tent, turning it white on the inside. I step back and watch him from a distance now. The more it snows, the more desperate he gets, trying to light a fire. The image turns surreal.

He strikes a matchstick, his face lights up for just a flash of a second, he grins, then a hard, biting wind blows it away. He does it once, does it twice, then a third time...each time he strikes the matchstick, the wind whisks the flame away! The Tibetan smiles a metal smile, his face flushed, his eyes red, fierce, a bit crazy!

I can see the blizzard rising in his head....

Suddenly in the entire wide expanse it is the Tibetan in his roofless tent, and me, with my camera, standing just outside, with not another soul around. The little boys who had been laughing and shrieking a little while ago are now nowhere in sight. Neither is the woman with the five yaks; nor do I see the little bridge across the river. Everything has quickly fogged out...the landscape is stark.

I'm now clearly petrified. I move back. My stance of a moment ago slinks rapidly into a zone of clear terror. I'm standing at the edge of his tent, just outside, unable to understand this...the children, what were they calling him? *Nyonba*...what is *Nyonba*? Tibetan word for...for...*mad*?

I shuffle the camera back in the case and start to walk away from the tent. The ground is now thick with snow. My boots make loud squelching sounds as I take large back-steps towards the barbed wires. The Tibetan follows me, frenetically flapping his arms about, a gesture I do not for the life of me understand. Then suddenly he laughs his pebble laugh. Is he playing with me or is he trying to frighten me? I begin to run. He growls, runs after me. The only thing on my mind is to somehow make it to the barbed wires, reach the tar road. Once I get to the edge and hurriedly squeeze myself through the knotted mesh, little white snowflakes spurt in all directions as the wire swings back in place. Breathless, I stand on the outer side of the barricade, the Tibetan on the inside.

I now begin to fast-walk towards the house in Agling, not once looking back. I wonder why the Tibetan has not followed me beyond this point. He just stands there in the sleet, behind the barbed wires, looking suddenly like a child lost, short-changed in the game!

'The ultimate source of the river Indus is in Tibet: it begins at the confluence of Sengge and Gar rivers that drain the Nganglong Kangri and Gangdise Shan mountain ranges'.

Sitting up late, skimming the Internet for information on rivers, I finally pull out the USB port and switch the light off.

I wake up again in the middle of the night with the same unease. It's that sound again, disturbing: the strange continuous drone of something blunted, yet sharp on the nerves. Jesus! This place is haunted! But I'm not afraid of ghosts. Why am I sweating in minus twenty degrees? I berate myself. If that little bukhari boy is not scared, why am I? I sit up in my bed. The glow in the heater has died out and the night around me is blue. Outside the glass window is the constant white fall of snow. Either I have been too excited, or been too tired. The sound comes closer.

All this must be playing up in my head. Maybe there *is* no sound out there and I am imagining it all! Extreme cold, they say, makes people hallucinate. But I am in a room, in a house with other people around, not out on a mountain pass all by myself, with the chill chipping at my ears. Why should I be hallucinating! I pull my feet out of the bed. There is no other movement around outside. I don't even hear the river, lapping. All is still, absolutely still, except for this one eerie sound. There it is, again! I stand up against my bed. I need to call out to someone. Slowly I gather the thick blanket around me, get my feet into boots and walk out of the room. Stepping down to the bottom of the staircase, I try and call out to someone, anyone, whoever may hear my voice at this unearthly hour.

'Hello! *Koi hai?*'

Downstairs everything is pitch dark. I now find myself standing in the middle of the hall, in complete blackness. I must get my answers tonight. Must find out where exactly the sound is coming from, but here there is no sign of life, neither any disturbance, for that matter. All is peaceful. The Ladakhi woman and her two children are sound asleep. They don't seem to be bothered by any sound, or even by the movement in the hall where I stand without switching on the light. All is still, not a sound...nothing, nothing at all...well, not any more. I must be imagining it then.

Back in my room I crawl back under the quilt and try to sleep my doubts away. Fifteen minutes later I am standing at the doorway again, trying to move my vocal cords, but I'm voiceless, I open my lips and shut them. I'm standing near the bukhari, the sound now just over my shoulder. Outside the glass-pane the snow continues to fall. I have to gather courage. If there is some *thing* out there, I'd better see it with my own eyes instead of cowering in bed from the dread of the dark. Maddened by my own fears, I suddenly leap and fling open the window.

'*Kaun hai?*'

A frosty wind whips my face, takes my breath away. Both arms flung out, I am standing peering into the white night. Then I see him...the lean figure of a man in a long red robe with straggly hair falling about his face. It's the Tibetan!

Skulking in the wintry midnight, rattling the silence of the old tar road, he is sauntering in the falling snow, dragging behind him on long strings tied to his waist, a bunch of empty tin cans....

Seeing a window open, a light flood onto the road, the Tibetan stops, looks up. I simper. He smiles. I wave. He beams. Huddled in my quilt I sit at the windowsill gazing at the road below.

The Tibetan lifts his arms, swings them around, turns, looks up at me again, and begins to dance...Like a dervish he twirls, the exultant spirit, laughing, his flaming red robe flailing about him in layers, his arms out-stretched; the tin cans held on strings, flying around him, jangling....

Sylph-like he dances, the Mad Tibetan, swirling on white earth....

I quickly grab my camera and rush back to the window, but then, I put it down. No, this is not a moment film can do justice to; this moment, I can only capture with my heart....

It's my last morning in Ladakh. My luggage is all packed and tucked in the back of the jeep. The Ladakhi family — my hostess with her two children — stand at the gate, waving at me. I ask the driver to take the old army road, drive by the riverbed.

As we take off, it gently begins to snow again and fog quickly moves in, fills the mountainscape. It is somewhere here that the tent should be, but I don't see much in the mist.

For a moment I glance back and see a trail of smoke swirling up towards the sky. I stop. The Tibetan seems to have managed to light his fire under the falling snow. Slowly we drive away from the river that flows with the secrets of the mountains in its heart. I can hardly see the barbed wires along the road anymore, neither the tent. He is far out now, somewhere in the mist, but I can sense him, out by the riverbank, standing besides his roofless tent...in the falling snow, the mad Tibetan, dancing....

Nyonba!

When he is fierce and wild, he's a bitter old man; but when he smiles, he's a child.

Life hasn't touched him.

⚘

D

It was one of those winters in Delhi when I like to prolong my stay under one pretext or the other, wanting to make the most of the cold weather, something non-existent in Bombay. But this time I have a genuine reason to linger on in the city since I have to make arrangements for the travel show we are planning to shoot in Himachal. I am the producer of the show and today is the only day left for getting all the last minute things done. There are maps to be picked up — road maps — and a list of PWD guesthouses in the district of Kinnaur, where the unit will stay for the two-week long shoot.

The three jeeps promised by Mahindra have already arrived. My Sumo is going to be the fourth vehicle but it has been sent for servicing. Earlier in the afternoon when I'd called the garage, I was told there was no driver today to bring the vehicle to Panchsheel Park, where I am staying with friends, and so I'd have to get it collected myself. Shucks! Who can I send now? The unit is arriving tonight by train; and the car has to be collected now! Now, before the garage closes down. I pull out a paper from my handbag and run through jottings in my black eye pencil.

Road maps – Himachal Tourism Office – before 5pm

Sumo – Panchkuiyan Road – before 6pm

Sari – Santushti Complex – this was done!

Trekking shoes – South Ex – done again!

Wet napkins, toilet rolls, ice-box, umbrella; all this will be Khan Market, on my way back, and...and of course, sunblock — 4 packs — also Khan Market! ...and stuff.

Got to rush now, first thing first. The road maps! Without maps, we are getting nowhere! Then, it would be Cottage Emporium, and after that I'll have to rush, rush, rush to get my Sumo out of that garage before it closes.

I rustle the paper back into my handbag and the next person I see on the road, I pounce: 'WHAT'S THE TIME, bhaiyya...please...?' my tone mellows in the second half, my eyes darting towards the right, looking for a taxi to flag down.

'Four-fifty,' and the man in the grey sweater decides to stand right there and stare at me. I have just about ten minutes to get to this office. I am already on Janpath, standing on the road outside Imperial Hotel, and this man here, staring.

I'd been told there'd be a taxi stand here, but I don't see a cab anywhere in sight.

'Chamko? Miss Chamko?' he says, finally figuring it all out.

'Yes.' I shoot a smile at him, which sends him away, grinning.

Phew!

Now, for a taxi to hail, but no, there's nothing. Maybe I should just walk it; after all, the Himachal Tourism Office is just across the divider on the other side. I can almost see the building from where I am standing. I decide to cross over on foot. The main road at Janpath is a pellet of traffic. Solemnly clutching my plastic bags I take one step onto the road, but get thrown three steps back into the sidewalk. Goodness! The traffic here is notorious! Worse than Bombay! I'll never make it on foot. Better to hail a cab.

Through the cacophony of car horns, the ruckus of motorcycles, the nuisance of autorickshaws, and even, suddenly, walkers, I see a black and yellow taxi speeding towards me. But it is towards the road divider; maybe there's a passenger already in it, but, never mind. I start waving vigorously, flashing my plastic bags up and down like a railway signal.

The taxi slows down but why won't he pull up on the left? How am I to get in with all this traffic zipping across my eyes? As I dodge my way through the chaos, tackling plastic bags in one hand and my purse and a leather folder in the other, my woollen shawl trailing all the way on the road, an autorickshaw screeches to a halt, right in front of my face, almost slicing my toes off.

'WHAT THE...Can't you SEE where you....'

I wish I had dumped these bags at my friend Pemu's place on Hanuman Road, instead of carrying them all around with me; I am sure to lose something. Irked at his clumsy driving, I nearly snap at the auto fellow.

'Uff! Don't you see that I...I...?'

'Crossing the road, Madam-ji?'

'Can't you slow down a bit when you see that I am....'

'Crossing! In the middle of the road! Why don't you cross at crossing! Over there! That corner!'

'Which corner?' I'm now losing it. I don't even care if people around me are recognising me.

'THAT corner, Madam-ji, There is also street sign! At signal! Signal made for crossing, like everyone else, cross over there, na!'

I look on my left, its far end blinking a yellow light. Cars are now honking, slowing down around the two of us — me, and this auto-wallah. But our argument has only just begun.

'You are educated na, Madam-ji? When we auto-wallahs do such things people yell at us, because we are illiterate. But look, Madam-ji, look at you! Crossing; in the middle of traffic! Then blaming ricksha-wallahs!

'I am NOT crossing! I am going to get inside that taxi!'

'Which taxi, Madam-ji?'

'That taxi!' I nearly lunge at him, pointing behind the man. 'Uff-fo! Now the taxi is gone! Look! It's GONE!' I fling the five bags up in the air and quickly try to grab them back.

The traffic now is careering itself around the two of us, honking, people swearing from car windows all around. Amidst the rumpus, two students, a young girl and a boy, they come up to me and stand, nervously, with a 'we know who you are' look on their faces, then a broad smile. Not now, please! Not in the middle of all this. Quickly the girl pulls out a notepad from her sling bag and shoves a clean white page between me, and my packages. I manage to smile back and pretend as if it is the most normal thing for me to be signing autographs in the midst of a traffic jam. Some of them are walking around, some pointing to others and grinning, 'It's her...it's her...,' recognising who I am. I tackle my shopping bags one more time.

'Ma'am! Please, can we hold your bags?'

'No, it's quite all right,' and I begin to scribble my name on the page between my chin and my shopping bags. Some more vehicles come to a screeching halt around me. The auto-wallah is now looking at me with new eyes; I am now a celebrity! Someone he should have *known*!

Suddenly his stance towards me changes, rather, his tone.

'Madam-ji, you are...you are....'

'Yes. I am.' I say with exasperation.

It is past five now and the Himachal Tourism office has most certainly pulled its shutters down on my life. What'll I tell the unit tonight? We are hitting the road at 6am tomorrow!

'Please sit, Chamko-ji! Sorry, I not recognise first, Madam-ji! Sit in my auto. I will drop you!'

'I just have to go across to the other side of the road....'

'I will take a U-turn from that end Madam-ji, drop you other side, no good traffic here to cross road on foot.'

I am without option here. Without thinking even for a moment longer, I gratefully dump my bags on the seat and jump into the autorickshaw that had nearly knocked me down. People grin as they see me riding away. The auto-wallah is now all excited, blabbering about Hindi films, driving real fast, zipping in and out of the bottleneck at the signal.

'This is India, how people love us here...where to go na, from here?' I am now sounding in my head, just like the auto-wallah!

I get off at the Himachal Tourism office, and begin to collect all my bags. I'll run to the third floor; hope there's a lift there.

'Leave bags here, Madam-ji. You go, I'll wait here.'

My bags with the Benarsi sari and my Tulsi kurtas. How should I trust this...I stop my mind from running in the wrong direction. He'll be here, I know it. I quickly drop the packages back on the seat and run toward the staircase.

The guy at the counter is already waiting for me, holding the road maps and other stuff. He hardly seems rushed, though the shutters are already half pulled down. He shows the maps to me, pointing to *points of interest,* wow! These are detailed, aren't they! Wait! And he pulls out for me a list of PWD accommodations along the Sutlej river belt, with a letter from their office, to use wherever we might find necessary. He then hands all this to me in a brown envelope and also some numbers on a piece of paper.

'Major Yadav will meet up with you at Samdo camp. He knows the areas you can shoot in. He will be guiding you from that point onwards.'

'Thank you... thank you!' I shove the maps into my large black leather bag and dart towards the staircase. Down at the gate I'm looking for the auto. Jesus! Has he disappeared with my bags? Oh, no! Not this now! I turn around to ask the watchman about the autorick... when I see someone familiar-looking — a lady — talking to the auto-wallah. He is grinning and nodding in the affirmative. Now what! What is he doing out there? And who is he talking to? I need to rush off to Panchkuiyan road for my car, for god's sake!

Seeing me he brings the auto around to where I am. 'Madam-ji, that lady, she knows you!'

'Yes, yes, everyone knows me. Now let's go, we have to get to Panchkuiyan road. Fast!'

'Don't you want to talk to her? She knows you, she says…from your school days!'

'My what?' I look up before moving out of the gate. 'From my school?' I ask the auto-wallah to stop. The lady, seeing me stop, walks up to the auto and stands in front of me. I am trying to place her. She stands there smiling at me. I know that smile.

'Remember me?' she says, 'from Sacred Heart School?'

I look at her trying to place her and know instantly that she is from my life — my good old school friend.

'Yes, yes, of course I remember…my god! It is really you? After all these years….' I could feel my pulse racing now for other reasons.

'It's been so long,' she says. 'You'd gone away to the US and we totally lost touch. Only the first few letters, that's all. Oh my god! I can't believe I am standing here in front of you; actually *met* you!'

'Listen, do me a favour…I'm a bit…in a bit of a rush. Listen, why don't you…? Wait, let me give you my phone…but I am leaving tomorrow morning for a shoot in Simla. I'm rushed but I…oh my! I need to talk to you…would you…would you hop in here with me? I need to get somewhere fast, my car has to be picked up, not too far, we'll get a chance to chat on the way….'

'Are you sure?'

'Yes, please come with me, we'll talk on the way! There is so much to catch up on!'

The lady hesitated a bit then smiling, she came and sat next to me in the auto. 'You can ride in autorickshaws? And no one recognises you?'

'They do…they do…normally I would take a…oh well, today I'm just too rushed. Tell me how've you been? Are you in Delhi? Do you live here?'

'Yes, I do…I live here…my sister…she was diagnosed with cancer, so I am with her now. I've left Dalhousie. That's where I had gone after school, remember? That's where you wrote to me a couple of times from New York.'

'Yes, yes, I do remember….' I'm trying hard to remember.

We look at each other warmly.

'You were in St. Patrick's House. You hated the colour green, you always wanted to be in the blue house; St. Thomas,' she spoke animatedly.

'Yes, I wanted blue…the blue of the sky…the blue of the sea!'

'You were fascinated by Picasso's Blue Period, remember? That's what you wanted to experience…didn't you, Deepti?'

I smiled, and a grin appeared on my friend's face.

'I hope you did not have to live it…Picasso's Blue Period?'

The auto turns at the corner of Panchkuiyan road. 'Madam-ji, where do we go?'

'*Bas*, just here…around that yellow board, where it says National Garage…just turn in there.'

My friend looks at me. 'You wanted to live for your dreams…and look where you are. You *are* living your dream! You wanted to be somebody, and you *are* somebody! I am so proud of you…so proud of the fact that we went to school together. I'll tell my girls that I met you…they'll be so thrilled! They've asked me often if you'll recognise me if ever I met you, and I have said of course, she will; she's my friend, we grew up together.'

The auto turns round the corner and waits for the red light to turn green. I start shuffling my packets, getting ready to get off at the garage.

'You do recognise me, don't you? You do remember me?'

I am caught off guard.

'Yes, of course. How can I not recognise you?' I blurt, the brown paper bags rustling in my hands.

The woman sitting next to me in the rickshaw is someone who'd been part of my life, I know that, but I am trying hard to recollect; recollect the little details she remembers. I too remember but they are not the same details; they are other details. I see her in her bottle green sweater with ink on her fingers, standing behind me in the drawing class, scared of Sister Jwenney, after ruining her watercolour paper.

'Are you sure?' she smiled. 'Let's see if you remember. What is my name, tell me?'

'Don't be silly! How can I not know your name? We've been in school together; you think I don't remember?'

My voice sounds false, despite all the effort I am putting in to convince her. I try desperately at that one moment to remember her name. For god's sake! It starts a 'D' as does mine, that I know for sure. But what *is* her name? I feel like kicking myself!

The woman looks at me with an unbelieving expression on her face. Suddenly it loses colour and the light in her eyes, is quickly gone.

'You don't...you *don't* recognise me, Deepti, you don't even remember my *name!*'

'No, listen I...I do remember...it's not that...I just can't seem to...please, listen....'

My mind is racing.... It starts with a...I know it! I know it!

I am trying all permutations and combinations starting with the letter D, but nothing...nothing...the last thing I hear is: 'I'm sorry, I bothered you.' In her eyes now I only see hurt, a kind of betrayal.

'No, listen!'

Before I can gather words, the woman has stepped down from the autorickshaw and is walking away into the traffic. I know it! I know her name, it is...it is...

'Daman!...Daman...!'

I am screaming after her, but she is quickly gone...lost in the crowd....

She was gone, 'my friend', gone forever...without believing that I had memories of her.

The traffic signal changes to green and the auto takes a U-turn and starts to drive away in the other direction.

'Madam-ji, is this the place?' The auto-wallah is now standing in front of the garage. I pick up my packets and pay him, my white Sumo all spruced up and shining, ready to go. I clear the bill at the counter, go and sit at the driver's seat, check the rear mirror, wait a minute for the engine to warm up, then drive out of the gate and onto the streets of Delhi.

Remember me? She'd asked.

Yes, I do, I'd said, and I hadn't been pretending.

 Thulli

August 1983
The Bombay monsoon

It was a blue — a turquoise blue — plastic curtain with white flowers on it; that's what had caught my eye in a window on Foras Road one August night, the heaviest of the monsoons in Bombay.

Our white Ambassador must have been quite conspicuous, going round and round the block in super slow motion. We had already done five rounds of the same street in Kamathipura, the red light district of Bombay city, when we realised it was well past midnight, and we weren't getting anywhere. I had managed to get three of my colleagues to escort me on my adventure trip. Inayat was at the wheel, while Tanvir sat in the front keeping a keen eye on undesirable elements. Crouched in the back, with a veil around my head, I was trying my best to be *not seen*. Uday sat to my left.

We were there on a mission. I was to play the role of a prostitute in a film, and I was here to do my *homework*.

It had been an unusually long drive into town, with the rain coming down in unscrupulous torrents. It was already half past ten when we started out from Versova. At several places along the road, the water levels had risen. The Tulsi Pipe Road was in utter chaos. By the time we crossed the bridge at Mahalaxmi and made a left for Saat Rasta, it was well past midnight. The area thereon was bleak and decrepit. People from roadside jhuggis squatted on the thresholds of shops, their homes inundated with water. Driving around Jacob Circle past a run-down structure called Hindoostan Mills, the Ambassador had managed to inch its way up to Maratha Mandir, bringing us to the outskirts of the red light district. But the traffic jam took us endlessly long to manipulate.

Caught in the deluge, people darted for cover, trying to flag down taxis and BEST buses. Autorickshaws, stalled in the rain, dotted the sidewalks. Stranded in the middle of the road, its wheels half submerged, was a yellow-topped Fiat taxi, causing the cram. Faces of actors and actresses hung folded on giant hoardings. All traffic from this junction had been diverted towards the inner roads and once we got to those, we had little clue as to how we could get back on track. None of us knew where exactly we were headed. The only name we had was *Foras Road*. From this point onwards, we'd have to ask for directions.

'Fau-russ Road?' The man under a sheer plastic gunny bag looked casually at Inayat who had his window half rolled down for directions. There was a hint of, not a smile, but more like a smirk, on his face as he said, 'Yes, yes, I know! That's where the women are!'

'But we…we are not….' Inayat, at once defensive, needed to give an explanation for wanting to get to the red light area in this deluge.

'Actually, we are…we are just….'

The man, without wanting to waste any time his or ours cut him short.

'At the light, go left. Two signals past, you turn right, come to big junction. Keep going straight till you see Dilli Darbar — large sign in bright red — that is Falkland Road, all *pros* area; you'll get what you want.'

The man under the plastic gunny bag seemed to know for sure, his way to the *pros* area so without hesitation, we followed directions.

The street that came up on turning the first left was quite run-down, also narrow. Here we had already started to see the first signs of the flesh bazaar. A man tottered out of a dingy joint, sozzled. A woman, soaking wet, stood at a taxi window bargaining with an Arab sitting inside wearing a long white robe. Slowly, we came to an open area, a major intersection, where the street had a signpost on the right but we could hardly read it. We asked a taxi-wallah if we had reached Foras Road.

'*Nahin, yeh* Falkland Road *hai. Woh saamne dikhrela na?* Dilli Darbaar*? Uske aage-ich hai sab...chhamiya!*'

As the car slowly cruised into the water-filled avenue, the lights in the area suddenly went out. I got a strange feeling. Though we were on the famous Falkland Road, it seemed very different from the kind of place I had expected to see. There was something odd here. It was pitch-dark and up in the distance I could see the neon sign of Dilli Darbar, un-lit. Though the road now was broader, yet it seemed like somewhere here, the world had started to close in.

The street we had now entered was completely dark, the only source of visibility being the headlights of our car. It was an eerie sort of feeling, driving through a lane, where you could see nothing; just the sense of something not being right. We drove slowly into the uncanny silence of the waterlogged avenue, broken only by the sound of ripples caused by the whirring of car tyres.

'Something tells me we should turn back,' Tanvir spoke gravely. No one said a word. Inayat drove cautiously upto the end of the lane, then, switched gears. Slowly, the Ambassador started to swerve, heavy with the water in its wake. This was when I began to get my bearings.

Thrown suddenly into the floodlights, as the car made a gurgling U-turn, on both sides of the street, were women, standing behind the bars, their 'powdered-to-white' faces alternately illuminating in the shifting light. They were neither soliciting customers nor bargaining. They just stood there; languid, confined within their cages, each occupying a separate dark world.

'Why are they locked behind bars?' I spoke under my breath, not believing what I saw.

'These are cages!' answered Tanvir. 'Women here are not allowed to get out.'

'They'd be killed if they did!' declared Inayat.

My god! So they do exist! The famous cages of Falkland Road; dark, squalid dwellings of the brothel women! I had heard about them, but seeing them with my own eyes, was something I wasn't quite prepared for. I felt as if I had entered a forbidden world. My gut feeling was to get away instantly but the anxiety I felt deep within me at that moment compelled me to stay on and see more. I hankered for the lights to come back on so I could get every little detail of my sordid surroundings. On the back seat, I sat on edge, staring into the dark, alert greedy, for *material*!

Women stood all around exposing their brown bosoms and bellies. Many were mere girls, eleven, maybe twelve; their faces pancaked to pink, clinging to the wrought iron bars, exposing bodies, with nothing yet *to show*. An old woman, her face painted a stale dead-white, sat on a bench at the edge of her caged world. As we passed by she suddenly stood up. I noticed that she was frail, petit and wrinkled. As her glance caught my roving eye, she unexpectedly smiled; the smile making deeper, the furrows on her withered skin. Something inside me, unsettled. Mockingly behind her, in full red glory stood the image of Durga, Mother Goddess, Shakti, the manifestation of woman power, her arms out-stretched, glittering against the dark, dank wall.

This was the most disturbing sight I'd seen in a very long time, even on film. I gaped at the old woman, then not quite being able to look her in the eye, turned my face away. Later on I realised that her smile, for that moment, had somehow made me, angry.

'This is an ugly sight. How can a man even think of...,' Inayat muttered.

'No, not ugly...it is sad, a sad sight.' Uday spoke with a pained expression on his face. He looked sucked in. I had gone quite speechless by now, given this feeling of slight unease in my stomach. My excitement for wanting to play the role of a prostitute was slowly diminishing. I tried to not lose completely, my enthusiasm for the role though inside I was in a state of disarray.

'This is not what we are looking for, Tanvir! It is far too depressing!'

I needed to get away from this dismal world of the cages. This was not what we had set out to see; not the role, not the film.

I had imagined *the flaring streets jostled by drunken men and bargaining women.*

I wanted to play a hooker with aggressive, sharp body language, something contrary to my screen image. To stand behind one of these iron bars and sulk, would be a cakewalk for me. I wanted a role that would challenge me as an actress. I wasn't going to cave in so quickly.

'Let's go, guys! We need to see *women in action!*' I straightened up, trying my best to motivate my team.

'Kamathipura!' said Inayat, before shifting gears.

We were now driving towards, Kamathipura what is known as the heart of the red light district. I reclined assessing my thoughts. The smile of the old woman. I wondered if I should have smiled back. I recalled the lipstick on her gaunt face running down the corners of her mouth. What was it about her that had unnerved me the most; was it her being *old,* or her being *there*; was it her *smile* that had unsettled me; or was it her being *resigned to her fate* that I found petrifying!

Driving away from the dark cages that night, I had little clue that just two years later I'd be drawing from that smile sitting on the floor before the camera, my feet turned in, playing *Kamla*, the adivasi woman resigned to her fate, oblivious of her own life's tragedy.

The rain had eased off for a while, turning to a soft drizzle. I don't know what streets we negotiated, but a couple of lefts and a couple of rights on the slushy avenues, and we were in front of Alexandra Cinema, known for showing foggy, run-down prints of old Hindi films. From here we headed towards Foras Road, the heart of the red light district. Once in the middle of it, we had no idea how to make our way through this labyrinthine world. The area was a maze. It was very late, nearly one-thirty in the morning. The streets, now half deserted, fell on all sides of the intersection called Shuklaji Chowk. There were lanes, inner lanes, by-lanes, back-lanes, straggling in all directions the sixteen lanes of Kamathipura.

We began to feel the rush of adrenalin once again as we entered the teeming quarters, murky tenements of garishly made-up hookers and sharp-eyed pimps. Flanked above the rows of shops on both sides of the lanes were the brothels; dark, dingy dwellings of fallen women their blue-green interiors neon lit. Some of the settlements were totally ramshackle, murky, reeking of decadence. Women of all ages, tartly dressed, stood huddled under the balconies, keeping themselves from getting wet in the rain. They were sitting silently in clusters at windowsills, standing on thresholds beckoning potential customers. Men promenaded the grimy exteriors of paan-beedi shops and mithai counters, looking for...meat!

There were a few customers still on the streets, walking uncertainly back and forth surveying the girls. Charged by the high energy and emotion of the blocks, I was all nerves, sitting on edge, my eyes darting on all sides, ogling at women. Aggressive looking guys peeped inside the car checking out my three colleagues. Spotting me, they'd quickly shrink back into the chaos.

I toyed with the idea of getting down and walking into one of the lanes, but quickly gave it up, as Tanvir retorted, 'Nothing doing! It is too dangerous; want to get killed or what!'

An autorickshaw — purple colour lit — pulled up at the corner of the street. A girl, dressed in a blazing red blouse and a white petticoat, her hair dripping about her cleavage, stood at a paan shop leaning provocatively against a pillar, hitting upon men, mouthing the choicest of gaalis moving her neck in a way that made the cheap trinkets dangle about her collar bone, her skin glistening in the neon light.

One scrawny, alert-eyed paan-chewing fellow stepped up from the sidewalk swinging a checquered hanky around his neck, gesturing for Inayat to lower his window. Inayat waved his hand in the negative, but the guy stood in the front, blocking our way.

'Talk to him...talk to him!' whispered Tanvir anxiously. Inayat rolled down the window. The guy in the lime coloured T-shirt plunged his dripping head inside, revealing a perfectly yellow-red set of teeth.

'Kya mangta hai, Saab? Bolo na! Ek dam jhakkaas maal dega! Tum log ke standard ka, Saab!'

He pointed across the road to a staircase where a woman in a dripping white dress sauntered towards us from across the street swaying her bare shoulders. The fellow looked back at my colleagues and grinned.

'Kya bolte, Saab? Teenon ko lelegi! Mangta kya?' Suddenly his grin vanished. The guy had spotted me crouched in the back. Disgusted, he withdrew his dripping head from the window, muttering, *'Baaju mein ek dhare-li hai, phir bhi idhar-ich ghoom-rele, saale!'*

I shrank. Uday looked sheepish. Inayat hurriedly rolled up the glass window. Tanvir turned around and gave me a dirty 'I-told-you-so!' look.

Tanvir had been most reluctant bringing me here; entertaining my bizarre idea of venturing out to the red light district.

'It is not a good idea, just not safe,' Tanvir had said earlier on in the evening.

'Drop it. Every actress playing a prostitute does not go around the streets of the red light district, it's far too dangerous!' This was Inayat, at his cynical best. But when my mind was made up, it was made up. I wanted to see with my own eyes; the real thing, the life of hookers, living in brothels, sleeping for money!

'I'm not going alone, am I? You guys are with me!' I argued.

'But tonight? In *this* rain? Mad or what?' Tanvir snapped.

'Yes! Tonight! *In this rain!*' I smiled.

I sometimes don't understand why my friends give in to me so easily. Tanvir was going to direct a film called *Red Light*, a sensitive, disturbing kind of subject; an incident that had caught my mind when I'd first read about it in a newspaper. At once I'd taken a cutting of the article to him. *This* was the role I wanted to play; the role of a prostitute! The story was dark, morbid towards the climax, but so what! That's life, isn't it? Tanvir's first film with me was called *Chirutha*, an NFDC production shot entirely on location in Kerala. In those days we had managed to can the entire film in just rupees three and a half lakhs! Apart from me, there was Inayatullah Kantroo, an FTII graduate who played my husband and Uday Chandra who essayed the role of my silent lover in the film.

I remember during the shoot how quickly we had bonded, and now we were like family, the four of us hanging around Tanvir's one-room-kitchen apartment on S.V. Road, engulfed in endless discussions about 'method acting', while his wife and his four kids slept through our animated arguments on *art versus commercial* cinema. This was my comfort zone. With the three of them around me, I felt quite safe.

We had already gone around the block on Falkland Road several times. Each time, the dark girl, standing slatternly at the corner, drenched to her skin, made lewd gestures at Uday and Inayat.

'*Aaja, saale! Dekhta kya hai! Aaja...lele!*'

Uday's face turned red. 'It's not a good idea. Let's get out of here fast.'

This was our fifth round of the same block. Now disgusted, spat the slut, '*Aaja, saale! Ghar jaake apni maa ki lega kya?*' which meant 'Come on, you...'...oh, never mind the translation!

'People are getting suspicious. Look...we are just going round and round...without *doing* anything.' Uday's apprehension was unfounded, I thought. But Tanvir and Inayat quickly went along without giving me a chance to disagree.

As we sped away, I heard the girl call out her shrill cries from the sidewalk. When I looked back at her, she was a beauty – unkempt and fierce.

In a strange sort of way I felt drawn to her aggression.

On our way back from Kamathipura I decided to take one more shot at Falkland Road, hoping to experience some interaction with the women in the cages.

Driving on the empty blocks past Charni Road and Grant Road, we now reached the first junction where the lights had gone out. It was three in the morning. On the right of the street was the sign clearly visible — written in white on a dark blue signboard — Falkland Road. We drove into it. Though the lights were back on this time the street had thinned out considerably. Past Dilli Darbar on our left, its shutters pulled down, and Gulshan Talkies on the right, the road looked somehow grimmer now, with no women standing behind the bars. All I could now see were blacked out holes, where sometimes a bright light threw into prominence, the existence of a cheaply decorated god smiling from the mantelshelf, oblivious of this *having-to-be-in-the-flesh-trade-with-no-way-of-escape* world.

'Where are the women? I want to talk to them!' I said, highly disappointed.

'Everyone seems to be done with all they had to do for the night, and finally have crashed out!' said Inayat.

'It's very late now,' said Tanvir, 'let's go home!'

'Okay, just one last round!' I pleaded.

A few straggling shops still threw green and mauve highlights across the wet pavement. Inayat drove up to the corner, made a left, then another left and we entered the same block again. Nothing. There was nothing. Then, slowly moving up the edge of the street, just before turning the corner, I saw a face; a woman sitting at a window, gazing quietly at the street below.

That face got me! Something about it; a sad, chinky face, against a bright blue plastic curtain. Before I could react or utter a word, the car had abruptly taken a right turn instead of the well-rehearsed left, and we were speeding away towards the suburbs.

Back on Grant Road. From there to Charni Road and then out on the seaside, over the bridge towards north Bombay. My sojourn with the women of brothels was over. Kamathipura was left behind and nothing 'concrete' had come of it.

I had barely slouched back into my seat, when I started feeling restless. There was something I should have done. I should have tried to meet some of those women, get to know them, something about their lives...I should have gained insight into their world, gotten *something* out of this trip!

'Too bad we didn't find anything much today.' Tanvir pulled at his cigarette and shuffled back into his seat.

But I had. I *had* found something. I straightened up. The woman at the window! The chinky-eyed woman. I should have gone up to her! Met her! *Spoken* to her!

'Never mind now,' said Tanvir, alarmed by my anxiety, 'we can always come back.'

'No, no, no, wait! Stop! Let's go back. I have to speak to her. I've seen her. She's there! At one of the windows.... I must meet her. Please...please...turn around. Let's just go back!'

'Where will you find her now? Which window? It is all dark out there. How will you know which face it was?'

'I will! I will! She was sitting against a blue…a plastic blue…a bright blue, plastic curtain…with white flowers on it. I will spot her. Just take me back on that road again!'

I don't think I gave the guys much choice. The white Ambassador screeched to a halt, vamoosed in reverse, splashed rainwater on empty pavements, sped back in the opposite direction. Even though they went along with me, I knew I was pushing the guys a bit too far.

Past the outskirts of the whorehouses, past the Arab gully and Shuklaji street, we were quickly back on Falkland Road, standing once more in the dark dreary street of the cages. The water level had receded and the rain mercifully had lessened. Falkland Road was lined with old wooden buildings. On the ground floor were the cages and above these cages, the buildings rose to three or four storeys, a few faces still visible in the windows above.

I was on the edge of my seat again, craning my neck to look up at the houses above. Now, where was the face that had caught my eye?

'Slow, slow…it was here somewhere, just before we turned left.'

Back to super slow careering of the Ambassador along the wet slushy street now emptied of customers. It was towards the end of the block where I'd seen that face. But above the cages, the windows were all shut. No men around either.

'Let's go home, it's no use. You'll never find her!' This was Inayat, fed up of catering to my whims all evening.

'You don't have to be so dismissive!' I was now snapping, already feeling guilty for having come back all the way from Kemps Corner looking for a face I did not know how, or where, to find. Stiff at the wheel, Inayat had manoeuvered the car twice back into the street, and stopped in the middle of the road. There was no sign of the chinky-eyed woman sitting at a window against a blue plastic curtain. I'd lost her.

'Let's go back...the street is deserted. It is not safe to hang around here.' Inside the car Uday was visibly uncomfortable. I sulked in the back seat.

'We should ask someone,' said Tanvir getting out of the car, looking around. At a narrow opening to a dark alley, two men sat murmuring in low voices. One of them was sloshed. The other was a sly looking scrawny fellow with a disinterested look on his face. Next thing I know, Tanvir is making conversation with the scrawny chap who undoubtedly looked like a pimp.

'*Kya, Saab. Phir se vaapas? Kuch maangta hai to bolo!*' the guy spoke with a '*Get out of here!*' tone in his voice. He'd obviously seen us go round and round all night without purpose.

Suddenly a window above where we stood, opened, flashing a bright blue plastic curtain with white flowers on it, flapping in the monsoon wind.

'*There she is*! Tanvir, look! She's there!'

Tanvir briskly pulled the fellow aside explaining something, pointing at the first floor window and then towards me. I didn't much care for the feeling I got at that moment sitting in the back of the car. Then, I saw the fellow's expressions change. He curiously moved towards me in a famous Dev Anand slant-step, bent his head to squint inside the half open glass, then grinning, he muttered,

'Yes, yes!'

Both the men stood a bit longer, negotiating. Then I saw Tanvir slip a note into the fellow's hand. It seemed like a while before Tanvir returned animated and opened the door of the car for me to step out, for the first time, in the red light district of Bombay.

'Come, you can go up and talk to her. He will take you there, follow him.'

'What did you say to him?' The adrenalin had returned.

'Nothing, I told him we are film people, wanting to make a film on the red light area. I told him who you were, and that you wanted to speak to the girl up there.'

'He's agreed?'

'Yes, only for a few minutes though, before their big Dada comes back! Now go, make it fast! Follow him up the stairs,' said Tanvir. 'We'll be right here, waiting.'

Visibly excited, also a bit nervous, I skipped towards the sidewalk. The man, amused, looked at me from top to bottom, then without changing his expression started to walk up a narrow wooden staircase, with each step sliding downwards. Now I was nervous. The creaky odorous staircase was too dark for my comfort, and the man with his enthusiasm, nearly fell backwards each time he climbed a step. Instead of feeling scared of him, my instinct somehow was to protect him, from falling.

Once up the stairs, the guy stood at the entrance door, knocking. The door, though open was barricaded by a half aluminium barn-like gate. This somehow confused me. I stood nervously behind him, almost not seen at first.

'Thulli!' the fellow called out. 'Thulli!'

A woman. Yes, the same chinky face stepped out from the dimly lit room, stood firmly in front of the pimp, and almost instantly started to brush him away.

'No, no more! Ikkey! Go! Go! No more! The girls are tired and sleeping. I cannot wake them up now.'

'It is *not* a customer, Thulli!' he said in a hushed tone, then moved aside shifting his light onto me, revealing me standing nervously behind him. The woman saw me, and for... for a moment there was in her eyes... not instant recognition, as I had expected, but disbelief. She suddenly looked perplexed.

'She is... she is....'

'She is a film star...,' and he whispered my name to her, bending real low, as if he was the only person who knew about my dark secret.

'She wants to talk to you. They want to make *a film on your life.*'

I at once shot a glance at him. Clever little fellow, I thought.

'At this time?' the woman lingered at the door, gauging me.

123

'Just for a few moments…,' I quickly pleaded, the *'please'* carried forward with my eyes. The woman relented. The man stepped aside allowing me to enter through the half gate.

'*Yeh Thulli hai!*' he said, introducing me formally to the woman from the window. The greater part of the room was in darkness; I walked into my grim surroundings, grateful for being let in at this unearthly hour.

I looked about the room. It wasn't much of a place. It was just a room, a single room, very small, cramped with two giant-sized wooden beds with bright coloured curtains hanging around them on strings. Underneath the beds, sprawled all over the floor were girls; 'Nine of them' Thulli informed me as she asked me to follow her. Then stepping adroitly over them she crossed over to the other side. I hesitated a bit looking down at my feet.

Bare legs zigzagging the floor, knees jutting into knees, hair enmeshed with hair, the girls slept soundly, huddled into each other. Then stepping over them, a knee fold here, the triangle of an armrest there, I followed Thulli avoiding placing my foot on braids collaged against the burnt grey cement floor.

Having managed this first bit, I now suddenly stood face to face with a distorted version of myself in the huge mirror tilted against the green wall. Appearing strange in this setting I saw myself slanted in the mirror — a cotton stole wrapped around my head, blue jeans and a white top, wearing my trekking shoes, the old olive Timberlands, refusing to wear out. A low night lamp turned to lime green, the corner where the cupboard was cemented into the wall. Both of us now stood in the only space left in the room that was the window.

'*Baitho,*' said Thulli, looking around for something for me to sit on.

From under a heap of bedsheets she pulled a red plastic stool spilling sleazy magazines about the floor. I tried not to look. She dusted the stool with it, then fixing her hair in the mirror, moved down on the floor, gracefully, I thought. I looked at the stool at first, then, decided to sit down on the floor next to Thulli, at the window.

Thulli curled up and smiled, the innocent smile of a child, I noticed. A woman of thirty or so, she looked older than her years. Her face had great beauty, I could see, with clear, clear skin and gentle features. Assamese? I inquired, looking for a start to a conversation.

'No, Nepali,' she replied, her legs pulled up against her chest. For a long awkward moment we looked at each other, then she spoke in awe, 'You are very famous.' Her Hindi had a *falling forward* tilt to it, I noticed.

'I have seen you,' she said gently.

'In a film?' I asked, my hopes rising. This was my chance of connecting with her instantly.

'No...not in film, on...the wall...on a poster...and on that!' She pointed towards a small television set, a grimy fourteen-inch B&W perched on a heap of aluminum trunks at the other end.

'You were singing...,'she said shyly.

'Singing?' I tried to restrict my voice to a whisper.

'Yes, under a waterfall...with...with Mithun Chakraborthy ... your song, "*uthaile ghunghata...chand dekh le!*"'

'Oh my god! You watch that stuff!'

'The girls watch it all the time. They love that song, they love seeing films; we get to watch them in the afternoons.... The minute they wake up, they switch on the TV set. I let them...they are young.'

'And you don't go to the cinema hall?'

'We hardly go out...!' and I noticed she held back. Thulli became quiet almost as soon as she said that. Dressed in a lungi and kurta, her knees pulled up on one side, she was far from the paan-spitting, hard-faced, *kaddak* madams of kothas we see in Hindi films. This was a face you would never expect to see in a brothel. I quickly revised my pre-conceived notion of prostitutes.

I looked about the room. Posters of film stars hung magnified on the green wall, the colours intensified, a Glaxo baby smiling amidst them. In the corner besides the wooden closet, glowing in the red night-light stood the image of Lord Ganesha, riding a mouse.

Thulli gazed at the street below, her head leaned against the blue curtain, her delicate Nepali features framed by white carnations.

'Are you not allowed to go out?'

'No, it's not that…but, where to go? How to get back?'

It was a sentence that startled me and I took a long time rearranging in my head the rest of my questionnaire. I looked down at the street where Thulli was gazing. A woman came out on the street running after a customer, abusing in the foulest of words she could spit out at him. One of the nine girls shuffled. Thulli showed no sign of disturbance on her face; she continued to gaze.

'How did you get here?'

I managed to ask the most clichéd question I could have come up with, without batting an eyelid: How did you get here? It was like being asked a millionth time, 'So how did you get into films?'

Without looking at me; Thulli smiled faintly, 'Everyone asks that — same question.'

'You mean the men? They ask that?'

'Yes, some. When they come first time feel awkward, you see they get nervous, doing it, right here in this room with all of us around, with just the curtains drawn around the bed.'

'You mean, this is where they have…?'

'Yes, this is where they do it. On the beds. This is all we have, these two beds…they take turns, sometimes wait in the staircase.'

I didn't know how to frame my next question. It was obvious.

'Don't you…hear them? I mean, the sounds….'

'We do…*lekin kya hai na, ji…*,' the same tilting forward expression in her voice again, 'they make sound all the time, but we don't hear anything anymore. At times the girls, waiting for their turn, take customers in the staircase. The younger ones, they are playing marbles under the bed while one of them is taking a customer on top of the bed. All sex happens here; around these two beds. Some of the men don't give a damn about any of us being around. They just draw the curtains and they think they are in private. They keep shouting abuses while doing it…all dirty-dirty words…they scream, but we don't hear them. Around these two beds, we continue to live our lives.'

I am, *zapped* is not the word. Thulli's face speaks a lot, but the words she chooses are limited. She tells me that she is the madam of this brothel, and all the girls and pimps call her Didi, as in 'older sister'. Sometimes there is a bit of competition among the girls, they share a strong bond, she and they are like her children she says, all nine of them.

The rain, intensified a while ago, now turned to drizzle, falling gently on our faces. For a while Thulli seemed like she wanted to ask me a whole lot of questions, but then, she simply smiled.

'What?' I asked curiously.

'Nothing,' and she smiled again.

'Tell me…tell, na!'

'No…nothing…once…once a rat got in here….'

'A rat?' I asked, having seen a little one crawl right under the cupboard a while back.

'Yes, a huge one! And it went all over the place…and…and….' Thulli began giggling like a schoolgirl.

'And what?'

'And…,' she started to laugh again covering her mouth with her hand, like the way I'd done in *Katha*, playing a simple girl living in a chawl.

'And the girls, they were petrified! The rat was like a cat! That big! Scrambling all over the place! And the girls, they were jumping over each other screaming, trying to shoo it away.'

'Then?' I could see where this scene was going.

'Then…,' Thulli's voice crackled. 'There were these two men, on the two beds with two girls…doing all kinds of huffing and puffing sounds. And the rest of them…the other seven also jumped on top of the beds, shrieking, falling over each other…refusing to step down.'

Thulli's eyes sparkled with tears, as she tried suppressing her laughter, recalling the bizarre incident. I was grinning, imagining this hilarious scene and decided it would be impossible to recreate it on camera.

The girls shuffled under the beds. One of them woke up muttering something, and seeing her Didi sitting with an unfamiliar girl — the two of us cracking up — went back to sleep again, muttering. Once Thulli stopped laughing, her face at once became sad. She was again lost in thought.

'*Bas*, this is where I like to sit, at this window,' she wiped the corners of her eyes, 'and I watch the bazaar from here. This is my world; this window and the girls, *mere bachche.*'

'Have you never thought of leaving here?' I was getting worse by the minute.

'And then do what?' Thulli turned around to look at me now.

'I mean, leave this profession and go away…to work in a home, as a maid or something?'

'I have thought, but no use thinking. When I was in college, I used to dream of….'

'College?' I nearly jumped, 'you were in *college*?'

'Yes….'

'Where?' I shuffled.

'In Kathmandu, for a year,' she curled up again.

'A year in college, and then you…landed here? Why?'

'I came here to Bombay thinking I'd find a good job. Actually there was no money for studies. There was no money to run the house either — no money at all — nor any food. An uncle from Dhulikhel brought me here saying I'd earn much more in the city than sitting on my parents' head. He said I was a pretty girl, I could do anything…modelling, even acting in films.'

My god! The same dream that brought me to Bombay city all the way from America….

'I have small brothers and sisters. My father drinks all the time and my mother cannot work anymore; she is mostly ailing and so I came here. But once I got to Bombay, I actually landed here, in this street, into this life. *Bas*, now nothing. There's no going back.'

A knock on the door disrupted our conversation. Thulli got up to see who it was. At the edge of the little half door, stood Ikkey, the pimp who'd brought me up here.

'*Chalo ab. Bahut ho gaya! Madam ko neeche bhejo! Apne ko koi lafda nahin maangta, samjha na?*'

'Yes, yes…she's leaving!' Thulli turned around, looked at the clock on the wall and then at me. It was four in the morning. 'You must go now!'

'Yes, I will…,' I whispered.

The guy stepped down into the dark and Thulli bolted the small lock on the door and returned to the window.

'There is a way, Thulli! If you want to,' I looked up at her. 'You can get out and make a life!' I must have now sounded typical, typical of one outside of this world.

'No…we can't…,' she said sitting down again. 'Only in films that happens. But in reality, no! Nobody will accept us outside of this world. *Once a prostitute, always a prostitute!*' It was Thulli's turn now to sound stereotypical, but the woman before me was delivering her lines without remorse or self pity.

No emotion, no drama.

Both Thulli and I were quiet for a while; each with our thoughts. Outside the rain had stopped. As we both sat looking out of the window considering the street below, the closed shutters of cages and the slushy sidewalks, the reality of Thulli's world slowly began to dawn on me. I looked about the room the girls on the floor, all

129

nine of them, the way they slept, coiled into each other as if tied together by an invisible umbilical cord held at the other end by their 'Didi'. Slowly it started to seep into my psyche, the actuality of their existence.

'The girls can't leave either,' Thulli spoke blankly. 'Nobody dares to. They'd just get beaten and brought back in here. The guys who keep us, the pimps — not this Ikkey but the other one, the big Dada, *bahut kaddak hai*! He's a terror, but he looks after us, takes money from the customers and then gives us enough to live, and we get by.... We enjoy *Chitrahaar* on the television, and watch *Yeh Jo Hai Zindagi* every night. I like Lajoji...we are happy here. No one wants to leave....'

Why was she saying this? I could not imagine anyone, any human being, being happy here. This, I was sure, was just her *defense*. This was certainly not the insight I was seeking; I wanted to trace something that 'rang true'...something that would lead me to the internal, provide a different perspective...something un-ordinary...or was I just imagining that it should be anything other than this?

My eyes must have given my thoughts away. Thulli turned to look the other way not wanting to say any more. This had been perhaps too sudden for her; a strange girl comes up this close, and begins to ask intimate questions. This wasn't easy for her, I could see but I had little time left. I had to get to the bottom of things. I had to know who she really was, what she felt, what she desired from life. This one-hour meeting was just not enough; I hadn't even touched the tip of the iceberg.

Obviously the real material lay underneath...all this, being just a façade. There was so much more, I could see. But how would I ever get to that? I was quiet for a long time. I did not know whether to feel sorry for Thulli and the girls, or to feel angry at myself, for not being able to probe into anything meaningful in this given time. I was sure if they walked out of here, no one would ever know where they'd gone; they could actually escape this, and find a life elsewhere. Fend for themselves through other means. After all, there were good people in this world! Someone was sure to help!

By now I'd nearly forgotten about my role and the film and also about the existence of my three colleagues waiting downstairs in the car.

Thulli looked at the wall clock. It was showing half past four. Before I left I wanted to say something, something appropriate, significant, something to change her world! I was groping for words....

Goddamn! My inability to say the right thing when needed!

Suddenly there is commotion. Thulli gets up with a start.

'It is Him! Get out of here! It is Him!' she jumps over the girls and stands at the door.

'Who? What? Who is *Him*?'

I scramble myself together, stand on my feet. Thulli is shuffling the small lock back into the rusted iron bolt. The voices in the staircase get louder, rougher — voices of men, arguing. I don't know what the panic is all about. I think I hear Tanvir but I'm not sure.

Something tells me I have overstayed.

'Go hide! Behind that trunk! In that corner!'

Have I heard her right? 'Thulli, who is it? Police? Is it the police?' My mind suddenly starts racing, on a *filmy* track. A police raid; headlines the next morning's papers:

'POLICE RAID IN RED LIGHT AREA! YOUNG ACTRESS CAUGHT IN BROTHEL!' No, it would be: 'RECOVERED FROM BROTHEL!' More appropriate: 'RESCUED FROM BROTHEL!'

Jesus! What the hell! This is bizarre! If it is the police they'll certainly recognise me. I am a known face! I will surely be able to explain my presence here. Is it such a crime to be doing your homework for a role? I try and be as calm as possible. The ruckus gets closer to us now, nearly at the door. Wait a minute. I can hear Tanvir's voice. Or is it Inayat? No, this is Tanvir. Why is he getting into a *panga* with the police? I can handle this myself! He will only worsen matters, silly guy! I walk up to the door and stand right behind Thulli.

'What is it? Let me see who it is. I can explain....' I tell her.

'No, PLEASE...PLEASE go hide! Don't come here! It is too dangerous! This man is....'

A man, thirty-ish, dark, large built, with blood shot eyes, wearing a white kurta and white trousers, barges in, beating violently at the rickety half door. In his right hand is a short club, the kind policemen carry in local chowkis interrogating small time criminals. He is completely sloshed, falling all over the entrance door.

Shit! This is no police! The man is a PIMP! The big Dada of the area everyone is petrified of!

'*Kidhar hai? Nayi laundiya!*'

Thulli hurriedly slides the lock into the rusted bolt, holding back the man with all her strength.

'No, Dada, please go away...there is no one here!'

The man continues using foul language, muttering things in his drunken state, but once I comprehend what he is saying, my blood freezes.

'I know a new girl has landed here. I will have her *first!* Before anybody gets his hands on her! It is *my* right to take her first! *Kaun saala* will try and stop me! I want her now! I want to fuck her! Now!'

My knees are suddenly giving way. I've never known fear of this proportion. I feel such a fool! Such a fool...coming up here, — taking such a big risk, here in a brothel at four in the morning. Tanvir had warned me! He had warned! Now what?

The man is clamouring at the door, pushing Thulli away to get inside. Thulli's strength will give way soon. *Then* what? Where are the other guys? Why are they not taking this creep away from here?

Suddenly amidst all the pulling and pushing, I hear my friend's voice. Tanvir, a small built guy is standing on the steps right behind the burly man, cursing him, flapping him from behind with whatever force he can manage.

Plastered against the wall to their left, I can't see the man, but I can see Thulli, I can hear her. She is holding the guy back with all the strength she can garner in her delicate arms, pleading, 'She is *not* for you, Dada! Don't mess with her! She is *not* one of us! She is a decent girl from a decent background. She is not here for *dhandha*! Please let her go!'

'Decent girl? You think I'm a *chutiya*? What is a decent girl doing in this *kotha*?'

I wanted to disappear, climb out of the window, do *something*!

Thulli's face fell, but her stance became stronger.

'I *swear* to you, Dada, she is *not* this kind of a girl. They are film people; they want to make a film...she just came here to talk to me!'

A girl wakes up and walks straight into the little toilet behind a curtain in a wall, pulls the flush, goes back on the floor and curls up again under the bed, not once reacting to the brouhaha, all this being nightly routine.

'Let *her* talk! To me! Let me *in*, you BITCH! *Saali*!' The man is so sloshed he can hardly stand straight. Yet he wriggles the lock out of the latch and staggers into the room, Thulli holding him back, standing in front of him.

'I *won't* let you touch her! You hear me, Dada? You are *not* going to touch her!' Thulli's stance is one of goddess Kali, her arms outstretched.

'Get away, *saali*! You will make enough money from her, but not before I have fucked her!'

I break into a cold sweat. Inside my chest I feel something pounding hard.

It suddenly dawns on me that this could be the end! That anything could happen here, tonight! Anything! That someone could get killed. That I...I...could kill someone! I start desperately

133

looking about the walls and floor for something to defend myself with; *anything* in the room to get my hands on. I was going to need it. But nothing...I see nothing...then, a bottle of beer, under the trunks with the fourteen-inch television set perched on it. I grabbed it and clung to the wall holding my breath. I wanted to kick myself for having the gall to come out to a brothel; at this hour! Fool! Fool!

I was in a state of shock, glued to the spot in the green wall. Thulli, while holding back the drunken man, was waving frantically at me behind his back, to get out of there, to *run*! *Run* for my life! *Run* before the man turned around and saw me. My mind raced fast. I had left my yellow pouch at the window, with all my notes in it. But never mind that. Thulli's gestures were large and frantic!

'Go! Go...madam-ji, RUN!' she mimed hard, her face distorting wildly.

Slowly I slithered against the grimy wall inching my way up to the door, praying, praying the guy won't turn around. The man's legs were now wobbling; he could barely stand. Thulli was holding him in her arms, his head bobbing on her shoulder.

'Come to *me*, Dada, *come* to me!' She was trying to cajole him away from me.

Seeing the man stagger, his body falling over Thulli's, I darted towards the door, but then, something, something stopped me...it was Thulli's words.

'I will give you *whatever* you want! Take *me* instead!'

I turned around and saw something that I had not expected to see.

'*Take me* instead, Dada! Let the girl go! Fuck *me*, if you want to fuck! I am here for you...your Didi is here. I will comfort you, my child...I will give you everything you need...come to your Didi...come, *mere bachche*! Come lie with me...lie with me...let me comfort you....'

I stood at the door, unable to move, choked by the scenario before my eyes. The man, ferocious a while ago, was now crumbling in Thulli's arms. I can never forget her face, the last that I saw of Thulli that night, as we looked at each other: *one woman to another*, our eyes glistening!

I slowly turned towards the dark staircase, then looked back one last time, at Thulli's world stunned by the dichotomy...the absurdity of the equation in human bonds.

Someone grabbed my arm in the dark; before I knew, I was rapidly being hauled down the creaky slanting steps, tripping all the way to street level.

Before I could get my bearings, Tanvir had flung open the door of the car and quickly I was shuffled into the back seat, the door slamming on my face. With a loud screech the Ambassador took off, driving insanely away from the streets of Bombay's red light area.

Inside the car, I...did not break down. None of the other three people said a word. No one turned to look at me. The rain had ceased. I rolled down the glass window letting the cool morning breeze soothe my face, camouflaging the brimming flood in my eyes. Inside me, I was shaking, from the last image I left at the door; Thulli holding the drunken man in her arms, pacifying him, cajoling...

'*I* will comfort you my child! I will give you *everything* that you want. Come to your Didi...come, *mere bachche*! Come, lie down with me...lie down with me...I will give you all that you need....'

...an image that would take a long time to fade from my memory.

 Balraj Sahni

The first star that shone on the screen of my real life was a tall, lanky, intense, and very polished man called Balraj Sahni. And he was terribly good looking.

It was the winter of 1963, the date, 3rd of November to be precise, when the youth festival was in full swing and my father, knowing my fascination for the performing arts, brought home two tickets.

'There's a group here from Bombay called IPTA, staging a play, *Kanak di Balli*. I hear that the actor Balraj Sahni is performing tonight.'

Two little ears perked up. *Kabuliwaala?*

'Would you like to see it? But there is very little time, we'll have to rush!'

My father was still speaking when I had already darted into my room. I had to quickly grab something warm to wear since it was going to be cold out there in the open...and my...my autograph book! I rummaged through the barsati room where my mother would shout at me each time she'd catch me cutting pictures out of the *Picturepost*, saying:

'Stop sticking those film stars' photos on your cupboard and get down to doing your maths! Your Sadhana is not going to pass your test for you!'

My autograph book! God! Where had I kept it? It was here in the drawer in my writing desk. And my socks! My socks! I leapt from my room on the terrace back to the gate, and before my father could finish saying what time the play would start... never mind, I was all set, in my socks and shoes, and bottle green blazer over my frock, two plaits dangling on either side, breathless! And ready to go!

The youth festival at Gandhi Ground was the big event in Amritsar every winter and would last a good ten days when people thronged from all over Punjab; from smaller towns and neighbouring villages to come and watch this festivity, sitting out in the open air auditorium during the fog-filled nights, munching peanuts and jaggery cakes. Allured by the medley of music, dance and drama competitions — a whole range of histrionics — the participants would congregate on a common makeshift wooden stage, displaying their talent before a raw, curious, non-judgmental audience.

It was love at first sight, with this tall, gentle, well-groomed, handsome man who stood looming before me. And me, down there somewhere, holding out an autograph book in my hand, looking wide-eyed at this amazing creature: an actor! An actor who creates magic on the big screen as the lights in Adarsh Talkies go dim for the matinee show; the face that ignites the euphoria and then stays back in your heart, forever! He was the one — *the first star that shone on the screen of my real life* — standing tall before me in his own skin. An image got imbedded on a young mind — an image called — *someone like him.*

I have little memory of the play. Having reached the grounds late we could hardly see Balraj Sahni, even though my father repeatedly showed the ushers the seat numbers printed on the tickets. But then, this was Punjab. There were no rules. First come, first seated.

I had imagined myself sitting in the front row watching Balraj Sahni perform at close quarters, but now I had to be content just listening to his voice over the loudspeaker. His voice was all that came across to me even though I was perched on my toes for the whole hour on the seat in front, to get a clearer glimpse of the actor on stage.

But once the play was over my father nudged his way through the crowd towards the back of the tented stage, holding on tightly to my hand. A crowd of rowdy boys had already thronged the backstage wanting a one-to-one encounter with the star of the show, to speak to him, to touch him, to check out if he was real, as he hurriedly stepped out of the makeshift green room, moving towards the door.

Balraj Sahni, as whispered around, was apparently in a great hurry to dash off to the railway station where he was to catch a train, the Frontier Mail that left Amritsar at ten-thirty in the night. There was no time. Tearing through the crowd, my father prodded me up ahead so I could at least get his autograph.

Tall Jats loomed all around me. My neck craned to get a glimpse of the star, to somehow draw his attention. It was difficult for me to find my way up to Balraj Sahni as he stood engulfed in the vociferous madness. My father and I managed to inch our way through the crowd and finally when we reached him, to my horror, I saw he was already turning around and rushing towards the exit.

'Can you give me an autograph, *please*...?'

I pleaded in a voice, which couldn't possibly have been heard by him in the din of the Punjabi language. I looked back at my father. His expression, looking at my face, was one of great empathy for the lesser mortals.

It was gone, my chance, I could see. The crowd had bottlenecked between me, and my dream man. I felt crumbled by fate.

But then something altered; a turn of destiny. Voices dropped to a low drone. People started to look back to where I stood. Through the knot of human faces, I saw Balraj Sahni turn around and walk back towards me. I could not believe my eyes! He had heard me! He was actually coming back, for ME!

'Autog . . ra...ph...' I mustered something like a voice again. The star now stood before me in flesh and blood, looking way below, where I stood, wide-eyed, gaping at him. Then, slowly he lowered his arm, taking the autograph book from my hand, and without looking at me, said, 'If I keep signing autographs, my dear, I'll miss my train!' Then looking into my eyes, he smiled.

'My dear!' he had said, hadn't he? 'My dear'! See? I knew it! He was someone *my own*! He had spoken to *me*, directly, amidst the entire crowd. He had addressed *me*, looked down at *me*, signing in my autograph book, in his own hand! I gazed at him, then at my notebook, where had written on the green page, in a blue-blue fountain pen ink, his name...B a l r a j S a h n i.

When I looked up at him again, the jostling crowd had already flooded in and torn us apart, the pandemonium of voices reaching a crescendo once again as the bright star disappeared into the winter night, the rabble at his heels.

But for me, I had trapped in that one moment, within my two little palms, a dream...a dream, for which I was going to live from now onwards. And I promised to myself...I promised I would be graceful like a Balraj Sahni...subtle like a Balraj Sahni. And no matter which role I played, or what I did in life, I would be genuine...like a Balraj Sahni, when I grew up to be an actress.

I still have that blue plastic-covered autograph book. I was nine then.

A nine-year-old, who knew what she wanted to be when she grew up.

Sometimes I wonder: If Balraj Sahni had not come to Amritsar, would I still have been an actress?

There are no straight answers. That is the beauty of life. I had learnt very early in my years to not look for straight answers. It is the ambiguity of things that enamours me, keeps me on my toes, or rather, in my boots. It is the un-known that fascinates me the most — the quest for what is yet to be discovered — that keeps drawing me back into living...and, like I always say:

To each, his un-known...

 Ruth Mayberry

The scene around Central Park South had monochromed to yellow ochre. Soon the streets of midtown Manhattan would be rustling with orange maple leaves strewn around by sudden gusts of the autumn wind.

Ruth Mayberry looked out of the window of her 55th Street studio apartment. Eighth Avenue bustled below her or so she imagined; the view through the glass pane was a bit hazy; almost fogged out, in the sense that it had an air of the *has been* to it; like in the old black-and-white Bergman film where time comes to a standstill and the protagonist is looking at his life from a completely different perspective.

Is it happening now, or is this an event in the past? Or is it not happening at all…a mere illusion?

'Oh! Screenplay!'

Ruth lifted the windowpane and stuck her head out, taking in a deep breath, filling her lungs with the cool October air. Wouldn't be such a bad idea to get that breeze straight on the face for a change. After all, how long would she remain cooped up in the tiny studio looking at life from a top angle? She took a few slow steps around the large peach-coloured, sink-in sofa, the only prominent feature in her room on which she'd often curl up in a foetal position and sleep like a baby. Then, sitting down at her desktop, she pulled out the keyboard and hit a key.

The scenario called *Memoir* came alive.

'You should change the perspective, Ruth. Tell the story from the actress's point of view. That way we'd have more juice on the page!'

Ruth was unable to digest that suggestion coming strongly from the agent; yet she rewrote the entire draft, tediously going over each scene, page after page, trying to make her script more *viable*.

And now, she felt she had short-changed herself.

She tried to close the 'working copy' but other stuff kept popping up: save this, save that, etc., etc. and she kept hitting 'no', 'no', 'no'. Finally, she slid the keyboard back into its place and switched off the computer. It was time to go for a walk.

She grunted a bit as she reached out for her black autumn coat hanging on the peg. Always black, she kind of complained to herself. She'd been wearing black for years now; it's this thing about living in New York City. She'd seen a whole generation in black, for generations, she thought. This winter she would need to go up to Filene's Basement and pick up thicker stockings. The ones she'd spent a packet on last winter were already quite gone.

Though she probably wouldn't need the umbrella, she might as well carry it. She reached out for the dark glasses lying on the makeshift dresser, with thick black sides; the kind that gave complete protection from the sun, for eyes that were hurting. Looking at herself in the mirror, she carefully slid them on, and turned the brim of her hat around to the front. Perfect. Black hat, black glasses, black coat, black umbrella; her hair could do with a little brushing though, and next time she must remember to tell the girl at the salon to dye it a couple-a-shades lighter than jet black.

Shouldn't the protagonist have been the other woman, the writer, rather than the actress? Like she had originally written? Wasn't that somehow a more interesting perspective? To see it all from the journalist's point of view! *Her* discovery of the diva's life after her suicide; *her* knowing about all the actress's secrets; *her* being thrown into a dilemma whether or not to reveal all those intimate details in her friend's biography which she was assigned to write, especially now that the actress was gone? Won't it be a terrible breach of trust? After all, that *was* the main point of conflict in the film, wasn't it? Yes, she would certainly go back to her original screenplay.

Six complete spiral-bounds sat above the hutch on the writing desk, all piled up neatly next to the row of dictionaries and Roget's thesaurus. Though the hard copies had her name on them, they were works she had either helped write, or co-written, or had been assigned to write developing someone else's ideas into full-fledged screenplays. But none of these six were anything close to the one screenplay that was closest to *her* heart; the one which was born out of *her*, was *her* baby, the one she had lived with for the past seventeen years, the one which would one day become her claim to fame!

Ruth waited outside the lift long enough to let a fresh flow of ideas take shape in her head. Then she pressed the lift button again and this time with urgency, but nothing moved. There wasn't that deep, grinding, metallic sound that preempts the coming of lifts in old Manhattan buildings.

'Oh heck!' She'd have to trudge down the six floors again!

For one split moment she was inclined to turn back towards the door and leave her rendezvous with the autumn breeze for later. But no, the minute she had stepped out of her cramped, tiny little apartment, her mind had already started to tick. Getting out was certainly a good idea, especially on an *emotionally happening* day like this one. Writers needed it; to be out there...crossing strangers on the streets, allowing themselves to feel, being vulnerable to life, being able to listen to their own heads...they needed it.

The first flight down was carefully putting one foot below the other, while holding on to the walnut banister in a way that anyone sprinting up or down the stairway may not be able to tell that the lady who lived alone in the sixth floor studio, known to sit quietly in the dark, writing film scenarios, could hardly anymore, see.

Ruth wasn't old enough to be sitting on a bench watching life go by, but there was this one spot in Central Park, on the corner of 59th Street and Fifth Avenue, which was her favourite. She could see Manhattan from an angle where the orange landscape spread before her like a copper flame; forever flickering.

Memoir was a story wherein the protagonist was a writer; a confidante, working on the biography of her friend, the famous actress, the diva of the Eighties, and being torn between the dilemma of saying, not saying, all that only she knew, that only she understood; all that, unless written about, may give a very distorted picture of the actress to the world. But one question kept hounding her: Was it right for her to say it all? Was it right?

The life of an actress is no big deal; it's about how she is perceived by other people, people around her; how *they* are going to remember her, and for what. But no, not at all, the screenwriter contradicted herself. Film stars are not about what they are to other people; they are about all the roles they play during their lifetime — the characters they impersonate on screen; that's what they are remembered for, not for who they are. So why should their personal lives be of such huge consequence to the world they emulate?

No, no, she must think this out more...this aspect has to be clear from the beginning. Whose perspective is it? That's the first thing her two years of studying screenwriting at Columbia had taught her; it was the one rule she was going to stick by. If she shifted perspective now, after seventeen years of having lived with the screenplay, it would be another film, not hers. And she had tried so hard...so hard, to somehow find someone, who would be able to understand the sensitivity of her writing and put in the money to make it into a feature film.

Last summer she found herself sitting at Sardi's having a drink with these guys from Washington D.C. While reading her screenplay out loud to them, the two young men kept going into wild raptures — simultaneously and at regular intervals — about the written word, without really listening.

'*AWESOME! AWESOME!*'

Ruth had given them a stern look or two at this most uncalled for, overly appreciative, gesture at the deeply disturbing and most poignant part of her script. But the two guys, programmed to react in a certain way when sent out for script reads, had no clue what stuff the lady sitting across the table was made of. Finally, Ruth Mayberry put her manuscript down, gulped whatever was left in her glass of red wine, and then, suddenly, laughed outrageously. Though the words ran through her head fast and high-pitched, she spoke slowly in a low growl:

'If you say "AWESOME" *one* more time, I'm walking out of here!'

The poor chaps didn't know what wrong they had done. After all, they only wanted to fund her project. But Ruth knew from that point on, as they sat tongue-tied and straight-faced till the end of the reading, the funds would not be forthcoming. So be it. For she would hate to be associated with...*morons*, was the word that came to her head at that point as she got up from the table, closing her blue spiral bound.

'I am a screenplay writer.'

Ruth spoke slowly in her usual gentle manner, and with grace, the one thing she never let go of. The man chatting with her at the opening night of the new art show at MOMA suddenly looked at the lady in the black hat, with refreshed enthusiasm.

'Really? Which films have you written?'

'I have written...,' Ruth's face clouded; she started searching for...words. 'I have written...not films...I mean, I have *written* many screenplays, but none have been made into a film...as yet.' She could hear her voice wane towards the end.

The man turned around to look at the painting again.

Her right eye had started acting up again. She felt a shooting pain between the eyelid and the eyebrow; a wrenching. She had never looked at herself any other way. She had always been, and would always be, a screenwriter! Who else *was* she?

'You are not a screenwriter unless there's a film made from your screenplay!'

Though the words had been harsh, they rang true.

She would, after working hours and when her eyes were okay, often walk down to Virgin Records on 59th Street and Broadway, six blocks away from her studio apartment, to pick up DVDs of recent films: *Inglourious Basterds, Brokeback Mountain, The Curious Case of Benjamin Button, The Hours, Across the Universe, The Good German, The Reader*, etc. etc., a couple of Oscar nominations, to study contemporary screenplay and understand today's cinema, something she felt compelled to acquaint herself with instead of hanging onto the old rules from *China Town* and *Godfather*.

Sitting on that bench in Central Park, Ruth recalled her days at Columbia studying screenplay writing. She saw herself as the lean, tall, statuesque young woman bristling down the streets of Manhattan, her head, forever ticking with scenes and dialogues.

'Would love to go through your script, Miss Mayberry!' said the head of Focus Films. 'Do send us a soft copy in Movie Magic, please.'

Movie Magic? Now what was *that*? She liked the term though; it somehow transported her back to her younger days, as a girl in Orlando, wearing her little purple dress going with her father to the movies, the regular Sunday classics.

'Stories to tell, Ruth, there are so many stories to tell. Movies bring us closer to life. They make us live so many other lives, other than our own, lives that we will never, otherwise, know or have an insight into. That's the *magic of movies*! Have you finished writing *your* little story, darling?

'Yes, Papa, I have written it all down,' the little girl would reply, walking hand-in-hand with her father, brimming over with joy in her lilac velvet hat. 'I love writing stories!'

Movie Magic, she found out from a friend over the phone, was this new software that young writers were using to submit their screenplays. It was technically more savvy than Final Draft, and preferred, almost a must, by most production houses. Final Draft, they said, was passé.

'Technically more *savvy*', Ruth mumbled to herself, trying to grapple with the challenges being thrown up in her face as she sat in front of her desktop struggling get a hang of the new, advanced, software.

'Oh, damn!'

Ruth's eyes were getting into the way of her reading, especially the right one. The doctors at Belleview had told her there was nothing they could really detect. But then, why had she not been able to see with her right eye even after the surgery? Another surgery? No, they had ruled that out, but perhaps they could have kept open that one option....

Ironically enough, after having quit being a bounce-board for an elderly writer living on the Upper West Side, she had taken up a job — a regular nine-to-five — at the Eye Bank down on Wall Street. The salary was good; she needed it. The organisation gave grants to needy people who required eye surgery. Ruth sat behind her desk in a lovely office with a river view, writing out cheques to well-deserving candidates, and here she was, sitting on all these grants, being well deserving herself, but none of the doctors knew what kind of surgery would cure her eye condition.

Now, if the word *irony* had to be re-defined, it would end up being spelt as r – u – t – h — m – a – y – b – e – r – r – y.

Any new ideas that came to her mind, for stories or scenes, even dialogues, she would immediately record in her little blue and silver dictaphone perched on her writing desk; always visible, right in the front, a reminder for her to record whatever her head spoke. The Screenwriter was used to making two-way conversations with herself. Many-a-times she would leave the recorder on, and forget. No, she was not going senile; it was screenplay, forever playing in her head.

'I'm going blind!' The dictaphone recorded Ruth's voice as she spoke to someone over the phone…someone who had called to have an inane conversation like, hi, howdy, etc. etc.

'It's my eye thing…I don't know what to do! I see less and less each day, you know…the doctors cannot figure out anything!'

The dictaphone also recorded her voice talking into the speakerphone about her ailment long after the person on the other end had disconnected the call, and the dial tone had come back on.

Ruth waited patiently for the agent to call and confirm her meeting with the studio head flying down into the city for the Foreign Film Festival at Lincoln Center.

'Make it work for me, Patrick; I'm no good at pitching scripts. You know I can talk endlessly about other people's work, but when it comes to selling my own script, I am hopeless.'

'It's a damn good script you've written, Ruth! What makes you think they're not going to just love it!'

'But Patrick, I've gone through…*Oh! So* many rejections!'

Ruth laughed abruptly and outrageously as she said that, making light of her own earlier apprehensions, trying to sound in a way that the young, enthusiastic patron of her art would not be able to gauge, that she was, actually of late, not very high on self-esteem having little hope left for her screenplay turning into a film.

Patrick was aware of those apprehensions. He knew, for instance, how Ruth had been so excited about her screenplay being auctioned in Philippines, but at the last minute, for some unknown reason, it fell out of the running. Yet, he believed in her writing. He had faith.

'Have faith in yourself, Ruth! These guys, they don't care about the commercial stuff; they want films with a *heart!*'

'But….'

'Shh! This time it's going to work! I have a hunch! Trust me! I can feel it in my gut!'

Winter set in dramatically at the end of November 2009, in all its glory, dazzling the streets around Madison Avenue with silver buntings and neon lights. Ruth walked slowly but surely with the help of her stick, refraining eye contact with people buzzing past her carrying bundles of gifts, rushing animatedly through swinging glass doors of designer boutiques on Fifth. She stood hooded under her umbrella at the corner where huge Christmas decorations were being craned up.

At the end of the street on Madison Avenue was the elegant Mont Blanc store. She stood, for a while, peering into the glass window admiring the sleek black pen with a gold nib displayed on white satin. If Patrick's hunch could even remotely be counted on, then she'd surely be able to buy a gift for herself this Christmas. A Mont Blanc was what she'd always wanted: *a writer's pen.*

Ruth walked to the end of Fifth and crossed the street at Park Plaza, overlooking Central Park. There, among pedicab drivers and cabs-in-waiting, she sat on her favourite bench overlooking the glittering evening skyline of midtown Manhattan. She hadn't even noticed that since the time she'd been living here, Manhattan had changed beyond recognition. It was now a splendid and exciting new world.

How she'd love to go back to *writing*…with pen, on paper! It was a *heart* thing. The few people who meant something to her, she would write letters to, instead of sending e-mails; write with her own hand: blue ink on white handmade paper. But then, that was rare.

The last time she remembered having *hand-written* to anyone, was this man — this writer from Greece — who had taken a fancy to her. They had been chatting for a while over the net, and finally, when he visited New York City, Ruth had felt like a girl all over again. He was all that she had ever dreamt of: gentle, caring, someone she could talk to. She loved him with all her heart and knew he felt much more than he expressed. When he returned to Greece he wrote to her, letters. They exchanged letters, in little sand coloured envelopes. He wanted her to come live with him on the Mediterranean coast, some remote island, he said, in Greece, in a quaint farmhouse with a wooden barn attached to it, something she could convert into her writing den, and write.

Oh, but this was years ago. She'd be, what, forty then? She had at once loved the idea and had gotten busy winding up her life in the city, quite not noticing, that the letters had stopped coming, and instead, had been replaced by brief emails. Abruptly, the e-mails also stopped appearing in the window of her Mac monitor…without explanation. And then, there was complete silence on the white screen.

Even now, at fifty-plus, those images refused to fade from her memory.

'Nothing dies,' she'd tell her friend Jeffery over the phone, talking long distance.

'Relationships live on, Jeff...they never die...they stay with you till the end of your life.'

Then later, there was this younger man at her workplace: this dynamic, young, ebullient charmer who made her laugh a whole lot...someone she'd fancied, fancying her, until the rude shock of reality hit her like a slap on the face!

It was her studio he'd been after; a roof over his head; and had wanted to move in with her for free! So she had turned out to be the perfect sucker once again, hadn't she? Allowing herself to believe that he could ever like *her*!

'An old hag' was how he'd referred to her in a dismissive tone, gushing over the phone with one of his ex-girlfriends. When Ruth confronted him alleging that he was using her, rather than being with her for love, he'd laughed and vehemently uttered the same words again — 'an old hag'!

If there was one thing Ruth Mayberry could not imagine compromising, it was her grace, her dignity. Though life had led her to it, she made it sound like her own conscious decision.

She'd rather be, without a man!

The screening of the Russian film at the Lincoln Center ended late. Then, there was this Q&A with the director, which couldn't be missed. Besides, with all those dignitaries present in the audience, and Patrick having promised to introduce her to the studio head, Ruth felt she'd let trivialities like being worried about getting late, or getting back, be dealt with later.

Someone pulled Patrick away, while the screenwriter stood with a glass of red wine in her hand, and a smile on her face, waiting to be introduced to the gentleman from Film Studio. The big guy, the decision-maker, stood in front of her, surrounded by the crowd, charming one and all around him.

'It's archaic, that stuff! And this, *Miss* Mayberry, since when did you say she's been writing scripts? Looks like, for the past seventeen years she's been writing the same script!'

The smile on Ruth's face vanished. Oops! She quickly pasted it back on, as if suddenly someone had caught her, naked.

'But with a name like that, I sure would like to meet her! Sounds more like a character I could put in my period psychological thriller!'

People around laughed. The world was a nasty place to be in.

Ruth Mayberry turned slowly around on her bad foot and looked for support. Someone rushing towards the washroom had left the swing door open, letting the draught right in... right in, so it chilled the bones. She shuddered. Slowly lifting her right hand and fixing her hat was the obvious gesture that came to her mind as a sort of rescue, as if her mere standing there in the room could be a thing, questionable. While slowly walking out of the hall where people jostled to get closer to the director and the producers, she tripped a little on her heel; then, moving towards the exit, she quietly placed the glass back on the table, collected her coat and umbrella before stepping out through the rotating door, and walked out onto the street.

Ruth's eye problem had started at the time New York City had the 'Big Blackout'. She had barely sat down on the chair in the doctor's chamber; her chin perched on the dip of the machine, his mini torchlight focused on her retinas, when suddenly her whole world went black. There was darkness everywhere, she could see nothing, nothing! Ruth had panicked. She hit about the doctor's chair:

'I've gone blind! Doctor, I've gone blind!'

Out on the street, the air was crisp. Limousines parked along the driveway quickly started pulling out at the end of the last show. A tall, lanky woman in black walked very slowly across the street with the help of her walking stick and stood at the corner trying to flag down a taxi. But at that hour, somehow, no one seemed inclined to stop. It was just thirteen blocks down, her block; she could as well walk the length. She started to walk.

358 West, 55th Street. Her last address had no nameplate on the door when they broke in early next morning, the ambulance sirens buzzing through the old red-bricked block.

Ruth Mayberry, a recluse, passed away quietly on the night of 11 February 2010 without causing a stir in the world she lived in. She did not leave a will. She owned nothing in life, except for her screenplays.

She had friends but they hadn't heard from her in the last six months. Losing the job at the Eye Bank because of her bleary vision was the last nail in the coffin. It seemed she was left with nothing to live for.

Zette, her old friend who lived in a large loft at South Street Seaport and whom she would occasionally visit, hadn't met her for a very long time now. Neither had Somi Roy, her Indian friend, the film festival curator. In fact, he hadn't seen her in years. The only calls she'd ever made since August last fall were ironically, long distance ones, to a friend named Jeffery Pavelka, living in Mexico City, who 'missed a loving kiss, a toast; missed brushing against her and hearing her outrageous laugh!'

Before walking out of her flat that night, Ruth Mayberry had gone into each and every file on her desktop, hitting on one single key for all that she had ever written.

Delete!...Delete!...Delete!

And then emptied the trash bin. She pulled down all her files from the tabletop and placed them into the fireplace, one after the other. Then, finally she picked from the hutch the script with the blue spiral binding, and carefully lowered into the fire, the only hard copy she had of her screenplay, *Memoir*. Then, taking a few slow steps, she drew back from the flames, sank into the large peach-coloured sofa and watched with complete detachment the scenes furl up into dark edges and rapidly light up in flames, her retinas reddening with seventeen years of dreaming and hoping.

The man was right. Where was she to fit in? All her life she waited to find her *place in the sun*, and now...was it too late? Was it time to make an exit? She decided she would not tell her story; she will not reveal to the world what it did not care to hear. Some things are not meant to be shared; some stories remain, untold.

Wrapped in a black muffler, a lady walked out into the bitter cold of the February night with the help of her stick, diagonally across the obelisk of Christopher Columbus, slowly dragging her bad foot through the diffused blocks back to the bench on the corner of Fifth. It was two-thirty in the morning. There was no one around. Manhattan seemed empty. Like in the old black-and-white Bergman film. No cars, no cabs, no people, no carts, no street sounds. Tiny lights still glimmered in the dark streets, reminders of the year gone by, of years gone by....

The night around the park cocooned her in a way that she felt somehow comforted. Ruth hadn't noticed how very gently it had started to snow. Soft white flakes fell like gossamers all around her on the bench where she sat; her stick tilted to one side; her dress, her hat, her shoes all filling with white. She loved the feel of snowflakes on her skin. Slowly, the ground was covered in a silvery white, a chrome-like image, shimmering in the nightglow.

Ruth could now see everything with lucidity. She saw before her eyes, her life rewind. She saw a photograph of herself in a white gown, standing on stage before an audience, holding an award, beaming! She saw herself in the barn studio in Greece, writing...she saw...kids.... She pictured herself walking down Fifth Avenue without her stick, sprinting through the crowds; her days at Columbia came back to her; then her childhood home, her father's image; she saw herself as a little girl, sitting by the window overlooking the maple tree in her mother's back garden, scribbling on paper with pencil, writing, stories....

A siren rang through the snow-laden streets of midtown Manhattan in the wee hours of the morning. A pedicab driver slowed down, as he peddled past a woman on a bench, on the corner of Central Park in a black overcoat and hat, sitting, still.

When Mr. Rodriguez, the janitor of the building, got the police to break open the door of Miss Ruth Mayberry's apartment, they found blackened sheets of carbon strewn all around the fireplace. On the computer screen, a message, sent by a Patrick Hague, flashed repeatedly:

HEY, RUTH!

YOU DID IT OLD GIRL!

THEY LOVED YOUR SCRIPT!

MEMOIR IS FINALLY GOING TO

BECOME A FILM!